THE MEDUSA PROJECT

HUNTED

Also by Sophie McKenzie

Teen Novels
Girl, Missing
Sister, Missing
Missing Me
Blood Ties
Blood Ransom
Split Second
Every Second Counts

THE MEDUSA PROJECT
The Set-Up
The Hostage
The Rescue
Double-Cross
Hit Squad

LUKE AND EVE SERIES
Six Steps to a Girl
Three's a Crowd
The One and Only

FLYNN SERIES
Falling Fast
Burning Bright
Casting Shadows
Defy the Stars

Adult Novels
Close My Eyes
Trust in Me
Here We Lie

THE MEDUSA PROJECT

HUNTED

Sophie McKenzie

SIMON & SCHUSTER

ACKNOWLEDGEMENTS: With thanks to Lou and Lily Kuenzler

First published in Great Britain in 2011 by Simon & Schuster UK Ltd

This edition published in 2021

Copyright © 2011 Sophie McKenzie

This book is copyright under the Berne Convention.
No reproduction without permission.
All rights reserved.

The right of Sophie McKenzie to be identified as the author
of this work has been asserted by her in accordance with sections
77 and 78 of the Copyright, Design and Patent Act, 1988.

1 3 5 7 9 10 8 6 4 2

Simon & Schuster UK Ltd
1st Floor, 222 Gray's Inn Road
London
WC1X 8HB

www.simonandschuster.co.uk
www.simonandschuster.com.au
www.simonandschuster.co.in

Simon & Schuster Australia, Sydney
Simon & Schuster India, New Delhi

A CIP catalogue record for this book is available from the British Library.

PB ISBN 978-1-4711-9873-1
eBook ISBN 978-1-84738-893-3

This book is a work of fiction. Names, characters, places and incidents are either
the product of the author's imagination or are used fictitiously. Any resemblance
to actual people living or dead, events or locales is entirely coincidental.

Printed and bound by CPI Group (UK) Ltd, Croydon, CR0 4YY

To Dana

'Synthetic life has been created in the laboratory in a feat of ingenuity that pushes the boundaries of humanity's ability to manipulate the natural world.

Craig Venter, the biologist who led the effort to map the human genome, said yesterday that the first cell controlled entirely by man-made genetic instructions had been produced.'

The Times, 21st May 2010

Fourteen years ago, scientist William Fox implanted four babies with the Medusa gene – a gene for psychic abilities. Now dead, his experiment left a legacy: four teenagers – Nico, Ketty, Ed and William's own daughter, Dylan – who have each developed their own distinct and special skill.

Brought together by government agent, Geri Paterson, the four make up the Medusa Project – a secret, government-funded, crime-fighting force.

After a disastrous spell in a training camp in Spain, the four have returned home to England with a changed understanding about their work and a new agenda . . .

1: OUT OF THE WOODS

According to Ed's map-reading, we were over halfway through the woods and had almost reached our destination. But Ed was insisting we waited.

'We can *sooo* make it to the rendezvous in two minutes,' I whispered. 'Three max. And there's no one here. Nothing. Listen.'

Ed folded his arms and listened. It had been raining for most of the hour it had taken us to reach this point, but the pattering drops had stopped now and the forest was totally silent.

I shivered in the cold, damp air.

'Hear that?' I said. '*Nothing.*'

'We have to wait,' Ed whispered.

'Why?' I snapped. 'There are no sounds. No movements. There's no one *here*. We're safe to move on.'

'Nico says to wait,' Ed said stubbornly. 'He says it's *not* safe.'

I rolled my eyes. Ed was such a doofus.

'Why should Nico know any better than me?' I argued.

Ed rubbed his forehead. His sandy hair stuck up in damp tufts, still wet from the earlier rain. 'Come on, Dylan,' he pleaded. 'That's the mission.'

I sighed and leaned back against the nearest tree. Technically, Ed was right. The four of us were on a Medusa mission to find and capture a fugitive hiding out in a hut in the woods.

Nico and Ketty were about half a mile to the west of us. We'd spread out in order to make less noise – and to be able to monitor more of the forest as we travelled.

We each had a job to do. Ketty's role was to bring on visions of the near future so we could avoid any potential dangers. She was trying to stay open to her visions the whole time, so Nico was letting Ed mind-read him remotely and passing on what she saw.

It was all kind of a stretch, in my opinion. Ed wasn't very experienced at remote telepathy while Ketty's supposed ability to see into the future was ludicrously unreliable.

'Look, Chino Boy,' I said. 'Ketty can barely control that freaky mind thing she does. It's real flaky. Half the time she can't see anything at all.'

'She's got a lot more in control of it since Africa,' Ed hissed.

I groaned. Ed was totally unreasonable where Ketty was concerned. Nico was the one actually dating her, but Ed *so* had feelings for her.

2

It was written all over his face.

'Well, whatever Ketty's seeing right now, we can't be sure that it's accurate,' I argued.

Ed folded his arms. 'I'll contact them again,' he said. 'See if there's any development. Okay?'

He turned slightly away from me and focused into the middle distance, trying to reach Nico through remote telepathy.

I shook my head. A few weeks ago I'd have had no problem persuading Ed to do what I wanted. Back when I met him, he was shy and gawky and hated his mind-reading abilities. Since then he'd had some real bad experiences. Most recently, we'd run up against this dictator guy in North Africa. Ed had tried to stand up to him and a girl he liked ended up being shot. All that would have been bad enough, but Ed expected the head of Medusa – Geri Paterson – to go after the man who'd killed the girl. Geri had refused, saying small stuff like that wasn't the government's priority.

Anyway, Ed got all worked up about it. And now he's insisting we pick our own missions.

Whatever. Who cares where we go or what we do? I love my ability – and any chance to use it.

Ed blinked, his connection with Nico presumably ending.

'What did Nico say?' I asked.

Ed took a few deep breaths.

'Jesus, Ed,' I snapped. 'I've known continents move faster than you.'

'Ketty and Nico both say to carry on waiting,' Ed insisted.

'But we've already waited for *hours*.'

At that moment it started raining. Ed shuffled sideways, under the shelter of the nearest tree. I didn't need to take shelter, of course. My Medusa ability means I can create a protective force field around myself whenever I want. It's like an energy around my skin. Great for stopping glass from cutting me and sticks from beating me – but also awesome for keeping my hair sleek and my make-up from running when it's raining.

Go ahead. Say I'm superficial. I couldn't care less.

'Did you at least find out what the danger is? *Why* we're supposed to wait?' I said.

Ed shrugged.

'So Nico and Ketty don't know.' I sighed. 'Don't you think they're being overcautious?'

Ed looked me in the eye. It kind of freaks me out when he does that. I mean, I'm not use to it. He didn't used to be able to make eye contact without mind-reading the person he was looking at, but now he's got all Mr Control about everything.

'No,' he said. 'They're not being overcautious.'

As he spoke, the rain grew heavier. I was having to focus hard now to stop my hair and clothes from getting wet. It struck me that if we were attacked and I had to concentrate on something other than my hair, it was going to get soaked.

The thought just about tipped me over the edge.

'Well, I'm not freakin' waiting any longer,' I snapped. 'The weather is totally gross and I can see the path up to the hut. There's nobody hiding in the trees. We'd be able to see and hear them – and there are way too many bushes and trees further out for any snipers to catch us.'

'I don't—'

'Oh, do what you want,' I snarled. 'I'm going.' And, without waiting for a response, I jogged off.

It was good to be running after standing still in the damp air for so long. I was still focusing on keeping the rain off me. I was aware of my ponytail flapping from side to side. I trod lightly along the earth path, my sneakers making hardly any sound. I kept my ears open in case there was – after all – an ambush, but as I'd expected, nothing was hiding out here.

Ed crashed up beside me.

'This is all wrong, Dylan,' he said, his voice tense. 'You're supposed to be protecting me. Not running off.'

'It's fine,' I said. 'You're okay, aren't you?'

'Yes, but—'

I pointed up ahead. There was the hut. We had less than thirty metres to go until we reached it – and safety.

'Let's get inside, then you can contact the others and tell them to join us,' I said.

I sped up, leaving Ed muttering behind me. We were almost there. Looking around carefully, I stepped off the path, my feet crunching softly across the damp twigs. Still

5

no sign of anyone or anything among the trees. I waited for Ed. He panted up beside me, looking cross.

At that moment the rain stopped. Grateful for the opportunity to relax my guard, I let go of the force field surrounding my hair.

Crash. With a thump, a man in a ski mask dropped out of the tree immediately ahead. He fired as he fell.

Bang.

I looked down, shocked, at the red stain on my front.

As I looked up, the man pointed his weapon at Ed and fired again.

'Bang,' he said. 'You're dead.'

2: ACCUSATIONS

The man grinned, then raised his radio to his lips. 'Mamba and Sidewinder are down, ma'am.'

Ed glared at me. I groaned, running my finger across the red paint that now splattered my chest. From the hut up ahead, Geri Paterson emerged.

Her thin lips were pursed tightly together.

The training mission had failed. Big-style.

And they were all going to blame me.

I turned on my heel and walked away.

'Dylan!' Geri shouted. 'Come back!'

I kept walking.

Next second the guy with the ski mask and the paint gun thundered up behind me and grabbed my arm, pulling me round. I considered resisting – using my force field to repel him – but what was the point?

'Come on, Dylan, I got you fair and square.' The guy tugged off his ski mask. It was Jez, our muscle-bound trainer, his face flushed with triumph. 'The least you can do is face the music.'

Whatever.

I let Jez lead me over to the hut. Ed was standing outside with Geri Paterson.

Neither of them were smiling.

'This is simply not good enough, is it, Dylan?' Geri said. Despite the fact that we were outside in a forest, Geri was still dressed like she was about to speak at a conference – in a dark blue Prada suit and heels. At least the woman had style, albeit a middle-aged version. She frowned, eyebrows raised, waiting for me to reply. 'Well? What do you have to say for yourself?'

'Everyone wanted to wait to approach the hut,' I said. 'But that was all based on one of Ketty's visions and we all know how unreliable *they* are.'

'So you thought you'd take matters into your own hands?' Geri shook her head and the pointy ends of her blonde bob jabbed at her chin.

I shrugged.

'I don't know why you're surprised.' Nico appeared through a gap in the trees, Ketty at his side. 'Dylan *always* thinks she knows best.'

I rolled my eyes. 'And you don't, I suppose?'

'But I *saw* Jez leaping out of that tree in my vision,' Ketty blurted out. 'Ed knew I had. I wanted you to wait until Nico and I got there. Nico could have dealt with him while we got Ed to the hut.'

I turned to Ed. 'Why didn't you say any of that? You made Ketty's vision sound real vague.'

'You need to trust us,' Ed said simply.

There was a pause. A soft rain began pattering gently on the ground.

I looked down. Truth is I have a bit of an issue with trust. Only idiots trust each other.

Why didn't anyone else understand that?

Geri cleared her throat. 'Ed, I don't think withholding information from a team member is the best way to build trust.'

I shot a grateful look at her. I've always got along better with Geri than the others have. She's hard-edged, for sure – and hugely ambitious. But at least she understands how the real world works.

'Don't blame Ed for this,' Nico snapped. 'It's not his fault if Dylan's a complete princess.'

I squared up to him. Nico's tall – and extremely good-looking, with dark hair and eyes and smooth, olive skin. But none of that intimidates me.

'What did you call me?'

'A princess,' Nico said, 'with a selfish psychic ability and an arrogant attitude that stops you from trusting anyone el—'

'I do trust you,' I snapped back. 'I trust you and your girlfriend to make stupid decisions and give stupid advice.'

'Dylan,' Ed said plaintively. 'That's not fair.'

'How *dare* you speak to us like that?' Nico said through gritted teeth. He seethed with fury. 'You've got no right to diss what we do. You're supposed to be in this team *with us*.'

Ketty put a restraining hand on his arm.

For some reason that gesture made me angrier than everything else put together.

'In this team *with* you? Don't make me laugh!' I shouted. 'I *own* this team. It was *my* dad who *created* the Medusa gene . . . remember? Who put it inside you . . . and he died a hero protecting—'

'He died in an *accident*!' Nico shouted back. 'You're just the same as the rest of us.'

I glared at him, a terrible wave of misery rising inside me at this angry reference to my dad's death.

I forced the tears back. No way was I showing Nico he'd upset me.

'That's enough, both of you,' Geri said firmly. 'At least I hope this experience has proved to you all you're in no way ready to be choosing your own missions. I mean, it's obvious you're not yet able to work as a team.'

'Why don't we just leave Dylan out of our next mission?' Ketty said.

'Fine with me,' Nico added.

They looked at Ed.

'My point is that you shouldn't be acting independently at all,' Geri went on. 'Surely you can all see that?'

Ed coughed. 'Actually, I don't,' he said. 'And while I agree that Dylan's a bit of a loose cannon . . .' He turned to Nico and Ketty. 'We'll need her for the mission I've found.'

I sniffed. 'Do I get a say in this?'

Ed looked at me.

Whoosh.

In an instant he was inside my head.

He's done that a couple of times before, but I'll never get used to it. You can feel his presence, even when he's not pushing to find anything out.

Right now he was darting in and out of my thoughts, preventing me from moving. Panicking, my thoughts shrieked out: *What the hell are you doing? Get out!*

Ed carried out zooming around my head. I couldn't tell what he was seeing . . . somehow he was blocking me from knowing what he was looking at.

Stop!

With another *whoosh* he was gone.

I turned on him, furious. 'What was that for?'

'I just wanted to know something,' Ed said.

'What?'

'It doesn't matter.' Ed looked around at the others. 'So you're definitely up for the mission?'

Nico and Ketty nodded.

Something shrank inside me. He'd already talked to them about it. They already knew what the mission involved.

And nobody had said anything to me.

'I've told you several times already, Ed,' Geri insisted. 'The mission isn't safe. And your performance today confirms that you can't be relied on to work independently. I don't want the four of you to do it.'

Great. Even Geri knew about the mission.

'What about *her*?' Ketty said, ignoring Geri and pointing at me.

'Yeah, do we *really* have to bring her along?' Nico snarled.

'I'm afraid we can't do the mission without her,' Ed said. 'If she'll come, that is?' He smiled. 'You will come, won't you, Dylan?'

All three of them looked at me expectantly.

I gazed at each of them in turn.

I guess if I was a different person I would have found it easy to smile and say I'd be glad to join them . . . that I was pleased to be needed and included . . .

But that's not my way.

'Sure I'll come,' I said, narrowing my eyes. 'The three of you wouldn't last five minutes without me.'

3: THE REVELATION

It took the three of them most of the next two days to do it, but Nico, Ketty and Ed finally persuaded Geri we should go on this mission Ed had found.

In the end I think she realised that, if she didn't agree, the others would do it anyway. And, if Geri was involved, she could at least provide advice and back-up.

I only knew they'd all been talking because Geri sought me out immediately after the decision was made.

Geri had always confided in me more than in the others. She knew my dad quite well and, though I'd never admit it, I liked it when she told me about their meetings all those years ago.

She found me in the backyard of the stone cottage we were staying in, staring out at the woodland beyond. We were somewhere in the North of England. Coming from America, I'm a bit vague on all the geography, but I think we might have been near a place called the Lake District. Not that I'd seen any lakes.

The cottage was quite cute in an olde English sort of way with draughty windows, flowery furnishings and cold stone floors everywhere.

I went out into the yard most evenings after dinner. It was easier than being in the living room with Nico, Ed and Ketty playing stupid computer games or listening to that dumb indie music they're all into.

It was a chilly night, but I was sitting on the swing seat in my retro pea coat and vintage Gucci gloves, enjoying the fresh, earthy night air and thinking about a pair of slingbacks I had my eye on.

In case you're wondering, I get a big allowance from my aunt and uncle in America. It doesn't make up for the way they've treated me but, hey, a lot of money's better than none, right?

'So what's this mission about?' I said, after Geri had made a few barbed comments about the others' pig-headedness.

Geri gave me that birdlike stare of hers. 'They still haven't said anything to you?'

I shook my head.

'Ed wants to investigate the death of a boy in a children's care home.'

'Why?'

'The death is logged as "accidental", but Ed's got it into his head that it was murder.'

'How come?'

'The official police report says a boy died after "an accident with a knife". Ed's got some hunch that the boy was

14

killed deliberately and that someone's covering up . . .'
Geri paused. 'I think after that girl he met in Spain, Ed has
a special interest in children in care.'

I nodded. Luz, the girl Geri was referring to, had been in
care. She'd been kidnapped by the people running the camp
we'd been sent to in Spain. Ed had really liked her . . . had
helped her escape, only to have to watch her die later.

I'd been there when it had happened. It wasn't something I wanted to think about if I could possibly help it.

'So Ed's on a moral mission to save kids in care, is he?'
I said.

'Mmm . . .' Geri sighed. 'Well, I won't pre-empt the
situation any further, dear. There'll be a proper briefing
tomorrow morning.'

'Fine.' I shrugged.

'You remind me more and more of your father, Dylan,'
Geri said in that clipped accent of hers. 'He'd get that
closed-off look in his eye, too. A man of few words and
very untrusting but, my goodness, when it came to his
principles, he stood up for what he believed in.' She paused.
'He didn't have many friends . . . I mean there were a few
scientists he worked closely with, and Jack Linden, of
course . . .' She paused.

Jack Linden was my godfather. I'd liked him, but he'd
ended up betraying us all earlier in the year. I reckoned
Dad was right to be untrusting. Jack Linden had been his
best friend, but he'd still risked our lives to sell the formula
for the Medusa gene my dad had developed.

15

'Of course,' Geri went on, 'your dad only really had himself to blame about the lack of friends . . . He wasn't an easy man.'

'He had my mom, too.' I turned to her, irritated. What was she saying? Some clumsy hint about how I should try to get on better with the others?

'Of course.' Geri shivered.

A minute later she made some excuse and went back inside.

I stayed out for ages thinking about my dad. After he'd realised the Medusa gene was going to kill the mothers of the babies he'd injected – including my mom, his wife – he kind of withdrew from the world. I guess he must have felt real guilty. I often wondered about the traffic accident he died in . . . Was he just careless crossing the road that night . . . or so preoccupied with his work that he didn't notice the car until it was too late? He was basically a genius and everyone says people like that often find real life harder than ordinary people.

And what about my mom? Was she cool with his being obsessed with his work? I'd never really talked about her to anyone. My stupid aunt and uncle only ever sneered about her. The most they'd said was that I looked like her . . . except for my hair and my colouring, of course. I have my dad's pale skin and wild red hair. Well, it would be wild if I didn't straighten it.

Eventually, the light went off downstairs and Jez appeared at the back door.

'Everyone's going to bed, Dylan,' he called out. 'You need to come inside so I can lock up.'

Reluctantly, I left the swing seat, went indoors and followed Jez upstairs. There were four bedrooms in our stone cottage. One for Jez and his girlfriend, Alex, who was our other trainer; one for Geri; one for the boys; and one for me and Ketty.

Ketty was already in bed when I reached our room, her back turned to the door. I was suddenly reminded of our argument in the woods earlier today.

Well, I wasn't going to be the first one to say something.

It was a while before I fell asleep, though it felt like I woke just seconds later – when the door slammed as Ketty left the next morning.

I dressed – in my ancient Juicy sweats and a totally gorgeous green jumper I got at Camden Market a few months ago. I already had on my mom's white-gold wedding ring – I never took that off. Next I put on my silver bangles. I usually wear them, too, though not if we're on a mission and I have to keep the noise levels down. Like the ring, the bangles were my mom's . . . very simple, very elegant, very beautiful. After I'd got the bangles on I messed around trying on a few different pairs of earrings. Eventually, I made my way downstairs.

The others were in the kitchen. Our two couples – Nico and Ketty and Jez and Alex – were sitting opposite each other at the table, like an episode of *Wife Swap*, while Ed and Geri were talking in low, intent voices by the sink.

They all looked up as I walked in.

I raised my eyebrows. 'What?'

'Ah, you're here, dear,' Geri said. 'We were waiting for you.'

Ed explained the mission – and my role in it.

I stared at him. 'It's just like the missions we've done in the past.'

'So?' Nico stood up. 'What did you think, that we were going on an expedition into outer space?'

'No,' I said, trying to sound as withering as possible. 'I just don't get why you all think this is such a valuable use of our time.'

'Of course you don't.' Ketty said.

Jeez, talk about prickly.

We set off after lunch. It was a long drive to the town on the English-Scottish border where the mission was to start. The first stage of Ed's plan was simple. Nico and I were to get us into the public records office just before the end of the day. After we'd broken in, Ed was to mind-read the person on duty to get that day's password. Once we had the password, we'd be able to get into the database of records and check out the report on the so-called 'accidental death' at the children's care home to see if there was anything suspicious about it. While we did that, Ketty was going to try and focus on predicting the next ten minutes for us, making sure the coast would stay clear.

Kind of a rerun of the training disaster in the woods, but with one significant difference.

'How are you going to cover our tracks?' I asked Ed. 'I mean, if you have to mind-read someone for a password, they're *sooo* going to know about it.'

Ed blushed. 'I'm using a new technique,' he said quietly. 'Kind of like a hypnosis thing that Alex helped me with. Stops people remembering they saw me, er, us . . .'

'So you've been developing your telepathy?' I raised my eyebrows. 'Way to go, Hypno Boy.'

I glanced at Nico. There was a time he'd have laughed at that. We used to be friends, but the more time we spent around each other, the less he seemed to like me.

Whatever.

'I still don't see why someone can't hack into the database remotely,' I said.

'Ed told you already,' Nico said irritably. 'They might be able to trace a hacker.'

'And they change the password every day,' Ketty added.

'Okay, okay,' I said.

At last we arrived at the records office. Jez and Alex were with us, giving tactical advice on how to behave once we were inside.

'If you get apprehended, say nothing, but let Nico disarm them, then put Ed in front of them straight away to block any memory they might have had of the incident. It's vital that you lay a false trail to cover your tracks,' Jez said, his face very serious.

19

'And don't forget your ABC,' Alex added. 'Attentiveness. Back-up. Caution. Keep your eyes peeled at all times. Remember to switch off your phones and . . .'

'. . . And never take unnecessary risks . . .' Ketty and Ed chorused.

'You remember how to get out of an armlock, don't you?' Jez added anxiously.

'We'll be fine,' Nico said impatiently.

'Yeah, enough babysitting,' I said. 'Let's go.'

The public records office was a large, square, red-brick building. Jez and Alex dropped us at the fire door round the back and we waited while Ketty tried to see into the next few minutes to find out if we would be safe going inside.

She stood there, her eyes all glassy, staring into mid-air. I waited impatiently.

After a few seconds, she stopped. 'I'm not seeing any problems,' she said. 'Looks like we're going to get in and out in about twenty minutes. The guy you're going to mind-read, Ed, is on the second floor.'

'Awesome,' I drawled. 'I feel *sooo* reassured.'

Nico shot an angry look at me. 'Dylan, there's—'

'Leave it,' Ketty said. 'She's not worth it.'

Charming.

Nico squared up to the fire door. With a swift flick of his hand, the thick metal bar lifted and the door opened.

I glanced around. Nobody was passing, or looking at us from any of the nearby windows.

I took a deep breath. I knew I had to move fast once we were inside.

I slipped through the doorway and looked around for the laser ray that Ed's research had suggested would be here. There it was, just one step ahead of where I was standing, its broad red ray monitoring the corridor.

I took a second to focus, making sure my whole body was shielded with my force field. Fully protected, I stepped into the laser's path, stopping it from reaching my body and picking up my presence. The others crept past, behind me.

Once I was sure they were safely through, I stepped out of the laser's path myself. We were in a dark, concrete corridor at the back of the records office. Voices sounded a short way ahead of us – the bored chatter of people leaving work for the day.

Ed pointed to a set of concrete stairs. They looked deserted.

'Two flights up,' he whispered.

We set off.

'No need to say thank you,' I muttered.

Ketty stopped us as we reached the first-floor landing, hissing a warning that she'd just had a vision of someone heading towards us from the third floor. We froze, but no one came.

I turned to Ketty, irritated. 'Are you trying to be annoying on purpose?'

'Shut up, Dylan,' she snapped. 'It's not that easy. I might

be out by just a few minutes . . . It's impossible to know for sure.'

Rolling my eyes, I set off up the stairs again. A moment later I found Ed beside me.

'Maybe it would help if you thought of your's and Nico's abilities as like doing maths or chemistry and our gifts – mine and Ketty's – as more like English or history. What we do isn't scientific or always precise. Just like in English there sometimes aren't right or wrong answers. D'you see?'

What a geek.

'Gee, thanks, Professor,' I said.

Ed shook his head and walked on ahead. He caught up with Ketty on the second-floor landing. They stood, discussing something for a second. Then Ketty beckoned me over.

'The guy Ed needs to mind-read is through there.' She pointed to a door marked *Level A Staff Only*. 'I saw him – he's working in a small office. Glasses. Dark hair.'

'Will I need to help out with my gift again?' I said, letting a seam of sarcasm run through my voice.

'No,' Ketty snapped. 'You're no use to us now until we leave.'

And again with the charm.

Nico beckoned us over to the *Level A Staff* door. He held up his hand, gesturing us to wait a second, then pushed the door open. Another corridor. Carpeted this time. We scurried past a closed door then, a few seconds later, burst into the office Ketty had seen in her vision.

It was tiny – furnished only with a desk and two chairs. The dark-haired, bespectacled man at the desk jumped up as we swept inside but before he could speak Ed made eye contact.

As Ed started to mindread the man, Nico turned to Ketty. 'Okay babe? Just keep your mind focused on near-future visions; I'll keep watch.'

Ed was frowning as he stared into the office worker's eyes.

'Something wrong, Ed?' I said drily.

'Yeah.' Ed sounded worried. 'I've got the password, but hypnotising this guy so he'll forget we've been here isn't as easy as I thought it would be.'

I rolled my eyes. 'What's the password?' I asked, scooting around to the computer. 'I'll log onto the database that we need to look at.'

'Okay. The password's *monitor636*.' Ed hesitated a second, gathering more information, then directed me onto the site we needed. I found the report on the 'accidental' death at the care home quickly. I only gave it a quick skim through, but it seemed obvious that Ed had been right and certain suspicious factors about the boy's death had been hushed up. I emailed the report to one of the coded Medusa email accounts, then deleted all evidence that I'd been on the computer. Of course anyone taking the trouble to search the hard drive might have seen that the file had been uploaded as an attachment, but if no one knew we'd been here, who would think to examine the hard drive?

I glanced over at Ed. He was still frowning. The guy he was trying to hypnotise had sagged slightly in his chair, but his eyes, though glazed over, still looked alert.

'Are we done?' Nico asked from the door.

'Yes,' I said.

'Not quite.' Ed sounded anxious. 'I'm still having trouble hypnotising this guy. I have to make sure he won't know we were here.'

'Well, that's awesome, Hypno Boy,' I drawled.

'Give him a break,' Nico snapped.

'Don't worry.' Ketty turned to Ed. 'No one's coming. Take your time.'

I glanced back at the computer. Ed had directed me to a national database of reports on UK deaths going back twenty years, since electronically stored records began. There were three sections to the database – one for murder, one for death by natural causes and the section I was looking at, for accidental deaths.

I'd closed down the search into the victim at the care home, but the national database was still live.

I twisted my mom's ring round my finger as my thoughts drifted to my dad. With a jolt, it struck me . . . my dad died fifteen years ago, within the time frame of the database, which meant that *his* accidental death should be on here, too.

My mind went back to what I'd been told . . . a traffic accident at nightfall . . . my dad stepping out in front of a car . . .

I looked at the others. Nico was still busy keeping watch, Ketty was still doing her freaky visions thing and Ed was still, clearly, trying to hypnotise the guy at the other end of the desk.

No one was looking at me. Even if they glanced over, they wouldn't be able to see what I was doing on the computer.

I pulled up a new search into the accidental deaths database and added my dad's full name: *William Hamish Fox*.

Two seconds later the response appeared: *Your search – William Hamish Fox – did not match any documents*.

I stared at the screen. That *had* to be a mistake. I typed the name again, this time double-checking the spelling.

Nothing.

Why didn't his name show up? I could only think of two reasons: either there was something wrong with the search function – which seemed unlikely as it had worked perfectly when I did the search on the care-home victim – or my dad's accidental death file had been logged in the wrong place.

My fingers were sweat-sticky against the keyboard as I moved the cursor to the next database: *Natural Causes*.

Nothing.

'How're you doing, Ed?' Nico asked.

He didn't speak loudly, but I was so absorbed in what I was doing I jumped.

'Nearly there,' Ed said. 'Just a couple more minutes.'

There was only one place left to look.

I turned to the murder database and entered my dad's name into the search box. A report flashed up immediately.

My heart lurched into my throat. What was my dad's death file doing here?

I opened the report, my hands shaking, and scanned it fast. I didn't . . . couldn't take in the detail of what I was reading . . . I just latched onto the bits that jumped out: my dad's name . . . his date of birth . . . the date he died, just a few months after I was born.

My eyes lit on a summary at the bottom of the page.

Victim: William Hamish Fox
Cause of death: murder CLASSIFIED
Assailant: CLASSIFIED

I stared at these words over and over.

And then, without warning, the file vanished. I tried to call it up again, but it had disappeared.

An icy shiver snaked down my spine.

'Done.' Ed pushed back his chair and stood up. I shot a look sideways. The guy he'd just hypnotised was sitting limply in his chair, head lolling to one side.

I looked back at the screen. Still blank, but there was no doubt about what I had read, even though it went against what I'd been told my entire life.

'Dylan,' Nico snapped. 'Are you listening to me?'

I hadn't even heard him speaking.

'Yes . . . no . . . coming.' I jumped up, my head spinning.

In seconds I'd closed the search, and logged out of all the databases. I switched off the computer and followed the others out the door as the terrible, inconceivable reality sank in.

My dad's file wasn't in the wrong place at all.

He'd been murdered and the true nature of his death covered up.

4: FAMILY VISITS

Everyone else talked non-stop all the way back to the cottage.

Ed was delighted that the whole plan had gone so well and full of ideas for what we should do next in the investigation.

Nico and Ketty were happy to join in, with Jez and Alex making suggestions as we drove.

I sat huddled in my corner in the back seat with my headphones jammed into my ears. I had my music on loud to block them all out.

Music helps me think. And I had a lot to think about.

I was in a daze at first. *Jeez*, if Nico hadn't pulled me back, I'd have walked into the laser beam by the fire door as we left. Not that I admitted it. Still, I got us past that and, once we were in the car and what I'd seen had sunk in, three questions burned in my mind.

Who covered up my dad's death?

Why did they do it?

And, if his death wasn't an accident, who killed him?

I *had* to find out.

We arrived back at the cottage halfway through the evening. Geri was clearly torn between relief that the outing had been successful and annoyance that we'd gone on the mission at all.

She kept nodding her head, her pointy bob swinging furiously back and forth, as we went through the debrief. I was careful to say nothing about what I'd seen. Geri had known my dad, so it was quite possible she knew the real circumstances of his death and hadn't told me the truth about it. However, there was no point accusing her of lying to me. She'd just clam up altogether.

No, I had to be cleverer than that if I wanted to find out what she really knew. Which meant I needed time to think.

Geri took a phone call towards the end of the debrief. She came back into the living room, a smug smile on her face.

'I'm pleased to be able to tell you that your family visits have at last been confirmed. Your visitors will arrive late this evening. We're putting them up in a local hotel. You'll be able to see them tomorrow – which means a day off lessons.'

The others were delighted. Geri had been promising us some time with our families ever since we left Africa two weeks ago. And who wouldn't want time off from boring school work? Alex kept us on track with all our subjects, like a tutor, and we had online lessons for certain classes, like math (which I hated) and languages.

Ketty clapped her hands together when she heard her parents were coming and Ed beamed at the prospect of seeing his stepmom and dad and sisters. Even Nico looked pleased that my Uncle Fergus – who was also his stepdad and the head teacher at our old school – was going to pay him a visit.

I'd only met Fergus a few weeks ago, of course, so it wasn't the same for me.

Geri turned to me. 'Now I know you hardly know Fergus, dear, but your Aunt Patrice is also coming—'

'You're kidding.' I stared at Geri. Patrice was the *last* person I'd expect to make the effort to visit me.

'Don't look like that,' Geri said. 'She really wants to see you.'

I didn't believe that for a second. I was sent to live with my aunt and uncle when I was two, just after my mom died. Aunt Patrice already had two children, Paige and Tod, who were a little older than me. I think she resented having another kid to deal with, though she certainly liked the life insurance money that I'd inherited.

Anyway, I never fitted in. I had my dad's last name and his pale skin and red hair while my aunt and cousins were all olive-skinned and dark-haired . . . plus, Paige bullied me from day one.

Next day, the families turned up one by one. Uncle Fergus was first. He smiled awkwardly and asked if I'd like to go out with him and Nico. I said I was waiting for my aunt.

Ed's family turned up soon after that. His parents were very ordinary – plain and plump, in horrible cheap suits, trying to look smarter than they were. I don't get the British class system, but I could see they were more than a little in awe of Geri. It was weird seeing Ed with his sisters. They younger one, Kim, was quite sweet, I thought, but Amy had buck teeth and glasses with horrid orange frames and never shut up. She kept staring around at everything, including me, going 'Omigod, omigod, look at that . . .'.

Ketty's mum and dad were smartly dressed, like Geri, but seemed real snooty, too. I was sorry to see they hadn't brought Lex, Ketty's cool, good-looking older brother, with them, but he was still in Singapore, where Ketty's folks live now.

Everyone arrived except Patrice. The three families set off separately for a bit of private time.

I spent the afternoon training in the woods with Jez – basic self-defence stuff to support my Medusa gift.

I was glad it was just the two of us. I couldn't bear the pitying looks Alex and Geri kept giving me when I was inside the cottage.

Patrice didn't show up until 6 p.m. She swept in, laden with designer shopping bags.

'Mwah.' She air-kissed me, throwing Geri a curt nod and ignoring Jez and Alex completely. 'Would you make a coffee for your poor, exhausted aunt, Dilly, honey?'

I gritted my teeth. I hate that nickname. It reminds me of Paige and years of torment.

'I'll make the coffee,' Alex said quickly.

She and Jez left the living room as Patrice sank into the large armchair.

Geri and Patrice chatted for a moment. They're quite alike in some ways. Patrice is a bit younger, of course, but she's all skinny with a pinched-looking face, just like Geri. And they're both super chic, in a middle-aged way. Right now Patrice was wearing a pair of dark jeans with a Chanel blouse and Hermès scarf and she smelled of something old and fruity – like an overripe melon.

I glanced at all the bags she'd deposited on the floor. Prada and Hugo Boss mostly.

'Nothing for you, honey,' she said, her lipsticked mouth puckering in pretend shame. 'I only had a few hours at the stores.'

'No problem.'

I wouldn't want what you chose anyway.

Alex brought in a mug of coffee and left. Geri made her excuses soon after, which left Patrice and me alone.

Aunt Patrice had already said she could only stay a couple of hours. Just as well. I didn't think I could have handled a longer visit.

As we sat in silence, my mind went back to my dad – and what I'd found out.

For the first time I wondered if my mom had known about the file that said he'd been murdered.

If so, might she have said something to her sister . . .?

'I've been thinking about my dad,' I said tentatively.

Patrice pursed her lips. Her beady brown eyes narrowed. 'And?' she said.

'About how he died . . .'

Patrice rolled her eyes. 'For goodness' sake, Dilly, what's the point in raking up that old business again? Your father was a law unto himself. He did what he wanted, when he wanted.'

Her voice dripped with contempt. I could feel myself getting angry.

'What's that got to do with how he died?' I persisted.

'I just mean he went his own way on everything. Not a thought for anyone else. He was selfish. Wrapped up in himself. Quite literally, which is how he came to walk out in front of a green light – he didn't notice the car coming.'

I perched on the sofa, trying to keep a lid on my temper.

'Okay, but how come you're so sure that it . . . that that's how it went down? How do you know he wasn't deliberately killed?'

For a second, the atmosphere in the room froze. Patrice's dark eyes widened.

'Who told you that?' she said, a deep, guilty blush spreading across her cheeks. 'Of course he wasn't delib— Dylan, what's got into you?'

I stared at her, my heart thumping. What did that guilty look mean?

That she *knew* he'd been murdered? All this time she'd known and she'd kept it from me?

I met her gaze.

'Why didn't you tell me the truth?'

'I *did* tell you the truth. Accidental death was the official version. The *police* said it was an accident, for goodness' sake,' Patrice protested.

'What about the unofficial version?' I said. 'Somebody told you something different, didn't they?'

Patrice looked away. Her sallow cheeks reddened.

'I can see you know something and you're not telling me,' I said, trying to keep my voice steady. 'So you might as well say what it is. It can't make any difference now.'

Patrice pressed her lips together in a thin line. 'I *really* don't see why you're so intent on—'

'He was my *dad*,' I said firmly. 'I have a right to know what happened to him. Or at least what people *thought*.'

'For goodness' sake, you sound just like your mother. Hysterical.' Patrice sighed. 'She once said she thought her phone was tapped.'

'Did she?' My throat tightened.

'Oh, that's just the start of it. She said that the motor accident was a cover-up . . . that William had been murdered. She was delusion—'

'Who did she think killed him?' I said. 'Why would it be covered up?'

I could hear my heart beating loudly.

'Your mother didn't know anything specific, Dylan, and I'm sure she was wrong. The whole thing was preposterous. I mean the *police* report said it was a traffic accident.' Patrice sat back in the armchair, examining her bright pink nails. 'Your mom was – as I've told you many times – prone to getting hysterical, especially at that time . . . You were just a few months old and not sleeping and she was exhausted, and before he died, your dad was completely wrapped up in his work and she was getting *no* help from him—'

'Please just tell me what she said.' I gritted my teeth.

'Goodness, it's so long ago.' Aunt Patrice paused. 'Let me see, she said William . . . your dad . . . kept going to the Hub . . .'

'What's that?'

'Some place to do with his work.' Patrice paused again. 'Not his lab, but . . . I don't know . . . a headquarters of some kind.'

'Who did he talk to there?'

'Geri Paterson at first, but Geri thought he was being ridiculous so he went over her head to her boss, but *he* didn't believe William's life was in danger either.'

'What was his name?' I asked.

'I don't know, but William was convinced that "the others" would come after him. After he died, your mom kept saying, *Now they have come after him . . . now they've killed him.* I spoke to Geri afterwards and she said it was nonsense. William was killed in a traffic accident. End of.'

I frowned. 'Who were "the others"?'

Patrice raised her eyebrows. 'Well, your mom didn't say, but I'd have thought that was obvious.'

I stared at her. 'Obvious?'

Patrice adjusted her Hermès scarf, tugging the two ends so they met. ' "The others" must be the others with the Medusa gene, of course . . . their families, I mean.'

'Why?' I said. That didn't make any sense. 'Why should it be them?'

'Because the families had just found out that the Medusa gene – which William had sworn blind was harmless . . .' Patrice sneered, '. . . was going to kill the mothers. I imagine William and your mom were convinced that they were going to take revenge.'

The room spun. I gripped the side of the sofa, suddenly light-headed.

My mom suspected my dad had been killed by the families of the other Medusa babies – the families who were, right now, in a hotel just a few miles away. The families of Nico, Ed and Ketty.

5: THE HUB

The little mother-of-pearl box was concealed under a sweater in my backpack. I took it out carefully. All my stuff – and everyone else's – had been left for a while at that hellacious training camp in Spain. It caught up with us eventually, but I hadn't looked inside this box for ages.

I was in the bedroom I shared with Ketty. She – and the others – were still out at the hotel with their families. I went over what Patrice had said, forcing myself to take an objective look at each set of parents in turn.

Firstly Nico. His stepdad, Fergus, was certainly around at the time my dad died but, as my dad was Fergus's brother, he didn't seem a likely murder suspect. My dad had left the only copy of the Medusa gene formula with him, which meant he must have trusted him. Anyway, I couldn't believe that Fergus, with his solemn eyes and straight-laced manner, was capable of murder.

Ketty had been adopted long after my dad died. She'd never known her father – and her mother, like mine, was now dead. If either of her parents had been involved in my dad's death, the trail would be well and truly cold by now.

Which left Ed. His dad had been around at the time.

Still, could he *really* be capable of murder?

I couldn't believe it. And I was even more certain that even if Ed's dad *was* involved, Ed himself didn't know anything about it.

Patrice had just left. Geri was working in her office and Jez and Alex were watching TV downstairs. The light through the window was dying as I glanced outside my room to make sure I was alone and opened the box.

It contained the few things of my parents that I owned. A white-gold necklace, with my mom's name – Ashley – hanging from the chain. I guess I could've worn it. Ashley's my middle name, after all, but something stopped me. I wore the wedding ring and the silver bangles, of course. There were a few photos, too – me and Mom and Dad. Dad had red hair and green eyes and a distracted look. Mom is much younger . . . and beautiful, with darker hair and pale, clear skin. Then there's me. I had terrible skin when I was a baby, all red and raw. Apparently, I cried a lot then, too. I wish there were some pictures of me with my parents that I looked recognisable in. Or at least some photos where I didn't look like the Devil Baby From Hell.

I flicked through the other items – an old Mac lipstick . . . a tiny vial of perfume that had long since lost its scent . . . some papers, including copies of my parents' marriage certificate and my birth certificate . . . and a little Tiffany appointments diary of my mom's from the year Dad died.

When Aunt Patrice first gave me the diary when I was about eleven, I pored over it for days, hoping for some insight into my mom's personality. But it was just a collection of evening dates with my dad and lunches with friends, plus a bunch of beauty appointments. I guess Patrice wouldn't have given it to me if it had reflected my mom's actual state of mind. She'd explained, a year or so later, how my mom had been sick in the head when she died . . . how she hadn't meant to do it . . . how it had been a cry for help . . .

It had taken me a while to realise she was telling me my mom had killed herself out of grief over my dad. Now, with a sick jolt, I wondered if my mom's fears that my dad had been murdered had driven her to suicide.

I caught myself in the mirror . . . anxious-eyed. Maybe Mom and I had similar shaped faces, but that was about it. I used to hate my own colouring . . . the way it made me stand out everywhere. But more recently, I'd come to like looking different. I loved the way people often did a double take when I walked past.

I turned to August in Mom's Tiffany diary. My dad had died at the end of the month – after which, I already knew, the entries stopped. I looked through the first week of the month. The appointments were mostly as before . . . highlights and a blow-dry on the 3rd, then lunch with someone called Laura afterwards, plus cocktails on the evening of the 6th. How weird that Mom's life was about to be turned upside down and she didn't know it. The note on August 7th caught my eye.

Another birth.
W to Hub

August 7th was *Nico's* birthday . . . He must be the 'birth' referred to.

I turned the page to the next week.

A meeting with her personal shopper . . . another lunch with Laura . . .

W to Hub was written again on Monday and Thursday and Friday. And again on the Monday and Wednesday of the following week.

That Wednesday afternoon was the day my dad had died.

Patrice had said the Hub was the headquarters of his work for the Medusa Project – and that Dad had gone there to speak to the guy in charge, Geri's boss, but that the man hadn't believed my dad's fears.

If I could find out exactly what my dad had said, it would give me a genuine lead. I knew from our Medusa Project briefings that notes were *always* taken in meetings . . . often recordings, too.

I just had to find out where the Hub archives were stored and access them.

I could have asked Geri, of course, but Patrice had made it clear that Geri thought my dad was paranoid, too. She wasn't going to tell me anything.

Downstairs I heard the front door shut and an excited chatter fill the living room. Damn it, what was everyone doing back here so soon?

My phone beeped at me. Absent-mindedly, I checked the text message.

My blood froze.

The text was short, but to the point.

We know what ur doing, bitch. Stop looking or u die.

6: THE BREAK-IN

For a second I felt nothing, then fear swamped me like a tidal wave.

My whole body shook and my breath just seemed to keep on going in and in. I stared at the text, the words burning themselves into my brain.

Who had sent it?

The message came up as blocked.

I let my breath out in a long, shaky sigh as Ketty and Ed burst into the room. Ketty was laughing. I jumped up, my face flooding red. The laugh died in Ketty's mouth.

'What's the matter?' she said.

'Nothing.'

Ed stared at me. Was he trying to catch my eye and mind-read me?

'Don't even freakin' think about it, Ed,' I snapped.

Ed raised his eyebrows. 'What?' he said innocently.

'That freaky mental thing you do,' I said.

'Jesus, Dylan.' Ketty glared at me. 'What's your problem?'

I almost blurted it out. But I was still in too much shock from the text to be able to talk about it.

'Nothing,' I muttered. 'What are you doing back here?'

'Our parents wanted to see where we were staying,' Ketty said.

Ed glanced at Mom's old Tiffany diary lying on the carpet at my feet. 'Why are you looking at such an old diary?'

I shook my head.

'Oh, it's your mum's diary, isn't it?' Ketty clapped her hand over her mouth. 'Oh, Dylan, I'm sorry.'

I glanced at her stricken face. *Jeez*, she felt sorry for me because I didn't have a mom and dad to take me out. The thought made me bristle.

'Whatever,' I said. 'It's no big deal.'

As I spoke, I remembered my earlier idea.

I took a deep breath. At least my body had stopped shaking.

'I was just looking at some of my dad's old stuff,' I said. 'You don't happen to know where the Hub was?'

'The what?' Ketty wrinkled her nose.

'It's where the original Medusa Project was based,' I said.

'Central London somewhere,' Ed said.

We both stared at him.

'Geri told us about it ages ago,' Ed went on. 'The Hub

was set up by the government to look into all sorts of unexplained phenomena. There were three teams – Geri headed up the one looking into psychic activity. Remember? Her code name was Medusa, that's why, when she found William Fox and backed his research, they called it the Medusa Project. The Hub was where all three teams were based.'

'Geri never told me all that,' I said.

'Nor me,' Ketty added.

'Oh.' Ed made a face. 'Maybe I mind-read it, then. Geri got me to mind-read her a lot a few weeks ago . . .' He turned to Ketty. '. . . While you went off to find your brother, remember?'

Ketty nodded. 'Why d'you want to know where the Hub was, Dylan?'

'No reason,' I said. I didn't want to explain. After all, if it *was* Ed's father who'd killed my dad, then I didn't want him or Ketty to work out what I was doing.

A moment later Nico turned up saying that their families were asking for them, so Ketty and Ed followed him downstairs. I lay on my bed.

What was I doing? Was I still going to go to this Hub building, check out the records of my dad's meeting with the guy in charge and find out who my dad suspected of being after him? Even after that vicious text I'd been sent?

My mind went over it again. *Stop looking or u die.*

I shivered. I had to go. I couldn't rest until I found out what, exactly, had happened to my dad.

Downstairs, Alex called out my name. I ignored her, my mind intent on how to find out the exact location of this 'Hub' without involving Ed or Ketty or Nico any further.

Another yell. Irritated, I swung my legs over the side of the bed and went downstairs. They were all there, standing in the hallway as I walked down.

Ketty was holding hands with Nico, her parents on her other side. Ed and his dad were next to them. All six looked up as I approached. Then Ed's mum broke off her conversation with Jez and Alex to turn and face me, too. I glanced along the row to the end, where Geri and Uncle Fergus were talking in low voices.

I looked back at Ed's dad. He was thick-set and square-jawed and, unlike Ketty's dad, looked extremely uncomfortable in his suit. Could he really have murdered my father?

Everyone stared at me.

'What're you looking at?' I said.

Geri stepped forward. 'You look nice, Dylan, dear.'

I glanced sideways, to the mirror that hung at the bottom of the stairs.

I guess I did look good – I was wearing a green dress that scooped and flowed over my baby. No make-up or shoes, but I had on Mom's white-gold wedding ring, as usual, plus her silver bangles and long earrings from the market that picked out the tiny sequins in the bodice of the dress.

The group around Nico and Ketty were all still staring

45

at me. I glanced at them sharply. Had they been talking about me?

Without thinking, I looked Ed in the eye, inviting him to communicate.

Whoosh. I felt him surge into my mind.

What were they saying about me? I demanded in thought-speak.

Nothing, Ed thought-spoke.

It suddenly struck me that I didn't want Ed anywhere near any of my thoughts.

Get out of my freakin' head.

Ed broke the connection.

I looked around, furious and humiliated, and hoping no one had noticed that little exchange. Ketty had, for sure. I could see her out of the corner of my eye, watching me warily.

Suddenly I felt overwhelmed. Tears threatened to well up for no damn reason. I forced them down and fixed my gaze on Uncle Fergus. Of all the people in the room, he was the one least likely to have hurt my dad.

'So how d'you like our shack in the woods, Uncle?' I said.

The words came out more harshly than I meant. Uncle Fergus looked slightly startled. I reached the bottom step and went over to him. To my relief, the others resumed their chatter. Geri turned to say something to Jez and Fergus smiled at me. *Jeez*, he had that same wary look in his eye that Ketty had just a few seconds earlier.

Why did everyone always look at me like I was on the verge of attacking them?

'This is a nice cottage,' Fergus said. 'How do you find it?'

'By remembering where it is when I leave,' I said with a grin.

Fergus looked startled. Again.

'Er . . . I meant are you enjoying it here?' he said.

Jeez. Why was this so difficult?

'I know what you meant,' I said. 'It's fine here. Awesome.'

There was an awkward silence. At least all the others were talking to each other, creating background noise. I twisted the ring on my finger.

'I remember your mother wearing that,' Fergus said softly.

I shot a look at him. He doesn't look anything like my dad – darker hair and eyes and without that wild expression my dad has in every picture – but there's something similar . . . something in the curve of his mouth . . . Maybe I didn't need to go to the Hub. Maybe Fergus had the answers I needed.

I lowered my voice, not wanting Geri to hear my suspicions. 'Did my dad . . . I mean, how was he before he died?' I said.

Fergus frowned. 'He loved you very much, Dylan. I don't know what—'

'Was he happy then, or worried about stuff?'

Fergus's frown deepened. 'Look, Dylan, I don't know

who's been talking to you, but you have to remember that your dad wasn't an easy man. He saw problems where there weren't any and—'

'You mean he was paranoid?' I said. 'Just before he died? Imagining people were after him?'

'Er, well . . . yes, he *did* imagine that and it really wasn't true . . .' Fergus looked extremely uncomfortable.

He was obviously hating talking about this to me.

He cleared his throat. 'We've just dropped in to see where you're staying, but we're going out for dinner soon. Would you like to join Nico and me?' he asked.

'No thanks.' I pretended to yawn. 'I'm totally whacked.'

A minute later the others started fussing and flapping over their coats. I went back upstairs. As I reached my room, I could feel Ed pushing into my head again.

What d'you want? I thought-spoke with a snarl. *You know this remote mind-reading of yours is a total pain in the ass.*

Just seeing if you're okay, Dylan. There was a trepidation in Ed's tone that was really irritating.

Why is everyone so freakin' concerned about me all of a sudden? I thought-spoke. *Why can't you all just leave me alone?*

I just remembered, he went on. *That Hub place you were interested in was in Great Portland Street – an MoD building.*

Oh, thanks, I thought-spoke back. *Why are you telling me?*

Because I know you want to go there . . . in secret.

Have you been sneaking into my head? I felt furious . . . then scared. What else had Ed seen? Did he know I suspected his father of killing mine?

I haven't mind-read anything. And I'm not mind-reading you now. I'm holding back, just sitting on the edge of your thoughts waiting for you to communicate with me. So no, I don't have a clue why you want to go to the Hub.

It's still real rude of you to—

I'm only trying to help. Ed sounded angry now. I'd only seen him lose his temper once before – when we were in Africa and that girl he'd liked – Luz – had been killed. *You know you might fool all the others with your tough-guy act. But I know you're not really like that . . . That's what I was looking for before, back in the woods after the train-ing mission you screwed up . . . I* did *mind-read you, then. I wanted to see what was underneath . . . and I saw the truth – you're just as vulnerable as everyone else.* His thought-speech softened. *So . . . so I don't mind coming with you to the Hub if you like – neither do Ketty or Nico.*

I hesitated, annoyed that he'd seen through me, but also aware he was offering to help.

Thanks, but no, I thought-spoke. *But if you can get Ketty to cover for me tonight, when you get back from dinner, that would be great.*

Sure.

And Ed, please don't say anything to Geri.

I won't.

He broke the connection.

I considered what Ed had just told me. If he was lying about the Hub address *and* knew what I suspected about his dad, he could be leading me into a trap. Jez was always telling us to have cover stories up our sleeves, so we could 'lay a false trail' if we needed to.

Maybe acting all helpful was Ed laying a false trail for me.

Maybe it was Ed who'd sent me the text warning me to 'stop looking or die'.

No, I shook the thought out of my head. Ed was no liar and I certainly couldn't imagine him sending me such a horrible message. Anyway, I was prepared to take the risk.

I sped up to my room, a plan forming in my head. Once everyone left for the hotel, I'd spend a bit of time chatting to Alex, who was staying behind with me, then pretend to go to bed early and call a taxi to pick me up from down the road. It was about twenty minutes to the nearest big station, then just over three hours to London by train. I reckoned I should arrive at the MoD building in Great Portland Street between 2 and 3 a.m.

That should give me plenty of time to find the records of my dad's meeting with the boss of the Hub – which would hopefully reveal who my dad suspected of trying to kill him. A genuine lead. And, with any luck, I'd even be able to get back to the cottage before anyone realised I was missing.

I waited for a non-suspicious time to go to bed. The next

few hours passed slowly, but at last I told Alex I was turning in. She nodded in agreement, saying that she was wiped out after all the families arriving that morning.

I went to my room, shoved a couple of pillows under the covers in case Alex popped her head round the door before Ketty got back, then jumped out the window. Jumping is *sooo* cool with my Medusa ability. I could hurl myself off a real high building and be fine thanks to the force field that protects me as I land.

Five hours later I was standing outside the MoD building in Great Portland Street. I'd already disabled the power to this section of the street. It's a neat trick – Jez showed me one day during our daily training sessions. You just find the power supply to the street, then burn through the cables. Obviously, most people would electrocute themselves doing something like that, but my Medusa gift protects me.

It was dark now, with all the lights out, and the street around me was deserted. I'd barely passed anyone on the short walk from the station – though there was still lots of traffic around, considering it was the middle of the night.

I peered down at the basement windows. They were, to my relief, not barred. The fact that they were also thick, double-glazed and clearly locked was not a problem. I selected a pane of glass. Staring into the dark room on the other side of the window, I psyched myself up, then punched.

With a sharp smash, the window crashed into pieces. I

tensed, listening for an alarm, but nothing. Good. Swiftly, I pulled out the biggest pieces of glass with my hands and scrambled inside.

Heart pounding, I crouched, listening for sounds, but no one was here. I smiled to myself. Nico might be able to open locks with a flick of his wrist, but being able to overcome fire, glass and electricity without getting so much as a scratch was even cooler.

At least, I thought so.

I let my eyes adjust to the darkness. I was in some kind of office area. A photocopier stood in one corner. There were desks and chairs everywhere, but no files on the shelves . . . no computers . . .

I headed out into the corridor, fishing for my flashlight.

There were three rooms off on the right . . . two on the left . . . I stopped, listening hard again. No sound. I was definitely alone.

I tried the first room on the right – a small kitchen. The next was a toilet.

The third was full of filing cabinets. An archive, if ever I saw one.

Resting the flashlight on the nearest cabinet, I took my art knife out of my bag and forced the drawers. Nothing remotely related to Medusa in either of the first two. I stopped, doubt creeping into my mind for the first time.

The original Medusa Project had been part of a top-secret operation into unexplained phenomena. How likely was it that the files – paper or digital – would be stored in an ordinary filing cabinet that anyone in the building could have easy access to?

As I thought this, there was a sound in the corridor. A tiny creak.

A footstep.

I froze, ducking back behind the nearest cabinet.

A bead of sweat trickled down the back of my neck. Holding my breath, I summoned my energy force field. I switched off the flashlight and the room was plunged into darkness.

Another footstep outside. Who was it? The police? Surely they'd have come in mob-handed with lights and noise?

Another footstep. I looked round. The edge of the cabinet wasn't big enough to hide me fully. But, short of moving the furniture, there was nowhere else to hide.

Suddenly a light was shining in my eyes. I dropped to the ground, but the light followed me.

Heart pounding, I rolled away from it, snaking across the floor. I reached the only table and rose to a crouch.

The light moved away, illuminating the filing cabinet I'd prised open and the files on the floor. Someone was standing by the door, holding a flashlight. A boy in a hoodie. Tall, slim . . . From the little I could see of him, he didn't look much older than I was.

'You've made a right mess in here, Dylan,' he said.

I gasped. How did he know my name?

'You might as well stop pretending that table is hiding

you,' the boy went on. 'Oh, and the police are on their way here – so you might want to think about leaving as well.'

I straightened up. 'Who are you?' I said.

'Cool accent.' I could hear the grin in the boy's voice, though his face was in shadow. 'I'm Harry. And I've got all the answers you need. But shall we leave full explanations for later? As I just told you, the police are on their way.'

As if to underline his point, the squeal of a police siren sounded in the distance.

Panic filled me. I raced to the door and turned left, intending to run along the corridor and climb back out the window I'd broken through earlier. Harry caught my arm.

'Not that way,' he hissed. 'The police will see you. Follow me.'

He set off in the opposite direction. I hesitated for a moment. Outside I could hear a police radio crackle into life. Two voices spoke in low murmurs.

What choice did I have?

I turned and followed Harry.

7: HARRY

Harry led me to the end of the corridor, then up some stairs to the ground floor. The building was empty and dark. We could hear the police officers in the basement below, stomping around. One of them was speaking into his radio mic, though I couldn't hear exactly what he was saying.

'Shouldn't we be trying to leave?' I whispered. 'Those guys are gonna call for back-up.'

'Don't talk. Move,' Harry ordered.

Torn between anxiety about getting caught and irritation at being ordered about, I bit my lip and kept walking. Harry led me up another flight of stairs to the first floor.

'Where are we going?' I hissed.

Harry stopped at the fire door at the end of the first-floor corridor. He stood for a second, listening for sounds downstairs. The policemen sounded more distant now, which presumably meant they were still in the basement. Harry pressed the fire-door bar down, then stood back.

'Ladies first,' he said. 'But hurry.'

'You are seriously winding me up,' I muttered, scurrying through the door.

Harry chuckled as he followed me out onto the landing of a fire escape. The stairs led down to the ground floor. Harry pointed to a fence just below us on the left, with a dark alley on the other side.

'Can you make that jump?' he said, a slight mocking note to his voice.

'Can you?' I was over the fire escape and into the alley in an instant, landing lightly on the balls of my feet.

Harry thudded to the ground beside me a moment later.

'Cool jumping,' he said.

'Thanks.'

'I meant me, Red,' Harry said, with another chuckle.

Red? Was that a reference to my *hair*?

Before I could say anything, he'd sped off again, only slowing as we reached the main road. I peered past him, round the wall. The police car, lights flashing, was parked out front of the building. There was no sign of the officers. Presumably, they were both still inside.

Harry tugged at my arm, pulling me onto the street. I followed him across the road. We took a left, then a right, running all the way past the underground station at the top of the road and across the much bigger, busier road at the top into a park.

Harry vaulted the park railings without any problem and darted into the shadow of some trees. I followed him, then bent over, trying not to pant too hard, as Harry leaned against the nearest trunk.

I stood up. 'Who the hell *are* you?' I demanded. 'How do you know my name? How . . . *jeez* . . . how did you know I was in that building?'

'Hey, Red.' Harry pushed himself up from the tree with a grin. 'Didn't your aunt and uncle teach you to say "thank you" when someone rescues you?'

I stared at him, dumbfounded again.

Harry pulled back his hood. The street lamp on the other side of the park railings shone across his face. High cheek-bones and dark hair. He was more interesting-looking than conventionally handsome . . . His features weren't precisely symmetrical and his nose was a little long while his eyes were set slightly wide apart. But there was something about him. Something that kept me looking.

Harry took a step closer, into even brighter light, and I could see that his eyes were a startling blue.

He raised his eyebrows. 'You look good when you've been running, Red.'

I curled my lip. 'Don't call me Red,' I said. 'And will you please answer my questions.'

'Sure.' Harry sat on the ground and patted the patch of grass next to him. I hesitated a moment, then sat down opposite.

'My parents worked with your dad,' Harry said matter-of-factly. 'Dad was in IT . . . Mum was one of your dad's research assistants. She was doing a PhD. They met, fell in love and had me.'

I stared at him. 'How old are you?'

Harry grinned. 'Exactly one year older than you.'

'Your birthday is the same?'

'Yeah . . . well, it's at the beginning of February,' Harry said. 'Just like yours. My mum was made up when your mum got pregnant . . . said they'd have so much fun being mothers together.'

'Your parents knew my mom as well as my dad?' I said. 'What are their names?'

'Laura and Jason Smith,' Harry said. 'Actually, our mums knew each other really well. They were good friends.'

I nodded. I couldn't place Jason, but the name Laura definitely cropped up in my mom's diary as one of her regular lunch dates.

'I think my mum introduced your parents to each other,' Harry explained. 'And they went out together as couples, too . . . before and after we were born. There's a picture at home of us playing together.' He paused. 'You look a lot better now than you did as a baby.'

I blushed, remembering the photos and the red-raw skin I'd suffered from when I was little. Then I felt annoyed that he'd made me blush.

'Well, all that's an awesome nostalgia fest for you, but would you mind telling me how you knew I'd be—'

'At the Hub?' Harry interrupted. 'My dad rang me . . . He . . . er, he lives abroad now. He said you'd hacked into the file on William Fox – your dad – in the murder data-base. He has some ace software that tells him when stuff like that happens. He said he knew it was you from the cameras in the street outside the public records office. He hacked those as well.'

I shook my head. 'How did he know I would come to the Hub?'

'He guessed that once you learned your dad was murdered, you'd ask more questions and find out that all the recordings detailing who your dad thought was after him were held in the Hub archives.'

My mouth fell open. 'And he sent you along to . . . to help me?'

'More to rescue you before the police arrested you actually. And to tell you that you won't find what you're looking for in that old MoD building.'

'So where will I find it?'

'Dunno,' Harry said. 'But I can tell you almost everything you want to know.'

'You *know* who killed my dad?'

Harry shook his head. 'No, but I know who your dad suspected. He told my dad all about it. And my dad told me on the phone last night.'

I stared at him. 'Why does he want me to know now?' I said.

Harry sighed. 'My parents thought you were better off not knowing the truth, but as you've found out that William Fox was murdered, they reckon you deserve—'

'Wait a minute,' I said. 'You're saying your parents *believe* my dad was murdered?'

59

'Of course.'

'They don't think he was paranoid and suspicious, like everyone else?'

Harry nodded.

I sat back, stunned. All my life people had been down on my mom and dad, saying that *he* was some sort of weirdo who couldn't cope with normal life outside his lab while *she* was neurotic and hysterical. Here, at last, were people who'd been their friends. Who had *believed* them.

'So who did my dad think was trying to kill him?'

I braced myself for Harry's answer. Would it be Ketty's family? Or Ed's?

'The others,' Harry said. 'The other scientists who knew about your dad's work on the Medusa gene.'

What?

'But—'

'They wanted to steal the basic gene sequence – the *code* for the gene – and work out how to copy it themselves.'

Other scientists.

I thought quickly back to what Patrice had actually said about 'the others'. She'd only told me she'd *assumed* Mom meant the others with the Medusa gene in their family.

'So my dad wasn't . . . didn't think he was being targeted by the families of the other people with the Medusa gene?' I said, relief and confusion rushing through me in equal measure.

'Not at all.' Harry wrinkled his nose.

'So which scientists did he suspect?'

'They're called Milton and McKenna,' Harry said. 'But Dad doesn't want you taking any more risks and going after them.'

'It's not his decision.' My voice rose and, despite the late hour and the danger we'd just escaped from, I struggled to quiet it. 'If my dad was murdered, I've got a right to know and—'

'Keep your hair on.' Harry grinned. 'I don't think you realise what you're dealing with here.'

'I want to speak to your dad,' I said, springing to my feet. 'He'll *have* to tell me. I'll *make* him.'

Harry snorted. 'Yeah, right. Listen to me, Red. My parents cared about your parents. They were gutted when they died. *And* when you got taken out of the country. Believe it or not, you really matter to them.'

'Then why've I never heard of them before?' I demanded.

'Who would have told you?' Harry said. 'I'm sure Jack Linden and Geri Paterson wouldn't want you anywhere near them. Remember, my parents are just about the only people who didn't think your dad was a total paranoid loony.'

'Your parents know *Jack* and *Geri* as well?'

'Of course. They all met Geri through the original Medusa Project and Jack hung out with them a lot. I met him once when I was little. He was really close to your dad when they were young . . . er, he's your godfather, isn't he?'

I nodded. 'I met him a few months ago when Geri brought him in to work for her,' I explained. 'But Jack betrayed the Medusa Project – he stole the Medusa gene formula, then tried to sell it to this big-time crook called Blake Carson. Afterwards, Geri Paterson had Jack arrested, so he's in jail now.'

I was hoping to shock Harry with this bit of news, but he just nodded.

'Yeah, I know. My mum and dad always said Jack was a chancer. But you're wrong about him being in jail. He did some sort of deal with the government a few weeks ago apparently . . . went off to another country in return for keeping quiet about you guys.'

'Oh.'

I was reeling. How could this boy I'd never met know so much about my life . . . so much that I didn't?

'There's something else,' Harry said. He gazed at me, his bright blue eyes intense. 'Apart from your mum, my parents were the only people your dad trusted.'

'So?'

'Before he was killed, your dad told them that he'd left the Medusa gene formula with his brother – your Uncle Fergus.'

'I know – that was the formula I was talking about . . . the one Jack stole.' I shivered, remembering how terrified I'd been when I realised what Jack was up to . . . and how the four of us had nearly died . . . how Ketty had even thrown herself off a cliff to save Nico's life. 'The Medusa formula was destroyed, then.'

'No.' Harry shook his head. 'There's another copy. My dad calls it the Medusa code.'

'What?' I said. 'How do you know?'

'Your dad told my parents he was leaving one copy of the Medusa code with his brother and one copy . . . somewhere else. That's why my dad really sent me here tonight. Because the scientists who were after the Medusa gene code fifteen years ago have found out that there's another copy and they're coming after it. My dad wanted to warn you.'

'Warn me?' I said. 'Why? I don't have it.'

'That's where you're wrong, Red.' Harry raised his eyebrows. 'Your dad left the second copy of the Medusa code with you.'

8: THE CODE

Harry's blue eyes pierced through me.

'You didn't know you have the code?' he said.

'I told you, I *don't* have it,' I said, more bewildered than ever. 'At least I don't see how I *can* have it. How could I have a copy of a complicated scientific code and not know?'

Harry shrugged. 'Dunno, but my dad says those scientists, Milton and McKenna, have just found something your dad wrote years ago which says you have it. So now Milton and McKenna are after you.'

I stared past him to the park railings and the deserted road beyond. It was a warm night, but the breeze made me shiver. I had very little that belonged to either of my parents – basically, just the items in my mom's mother-of-pearl box. They'd died so long ago . . . I couldn't imagine what this note of my dad's could say or where the code for the Medusa gene could be – or why anyone would be so convinced that it was definitely still in my possession.

'So I'm being hunted for something I don't understand and can't locate.'

Harry stood up and held out his hand to help me. 'That about sums it up, Red.'

I took his hand, irritated. 'I told you, don't call me that.'

Harry grinned as he pulled me up. I stumbled as I rose, bumping against him. My cheek brushed against his shoulder. I could smell the soap he used, feel the rough cotton of his jacket.

I gripped his arm to steady myself and looked up. He was staring at me, our faces close together.

Too close.

I pulled away, my force field automatically turning on.

Harry looked at me, puzzled. 'What's up?'

'Nothing.' I released the force field. 'I should get back to the station.'

I desperately wanted to be on my own, to have time to think.

'Sure.' Harry walked towards the fence. 'So what's it like having this Medusa gene? Has it kicked in properly yet?'

I suddenly wanted to impress him with my ability. 'Yeah,' I said. 'I'll show you. Hit me.'

'What?' He stared at me.

'Go on,' I said. 'Try and hit me. Punch my face.'

Harry took a step back, shaking his head. 'No,' he said.

He looked really alarmed. I swallowed. *Jeez*, I was messing up.

'Okay.' I looked around, determined to find something to impress him with. 'Look.'

I hauled myself onto the fence and scrambled to the top. Then I turned around. 'Watch this.' I let myself fall backwards, force field engaged. In the second before I landed on my back, unharmed, I heard Harry gasp.

I shut my eyes as he hurdled over the fence himself. He landed lightly on the pavement and rushed over. I could feel him kneeling beside me, his face close to mine again. 'Dylan? Are you all right? Dylan?'

I opened my eyes. He was right there, his face next to mine, dark hair falling over those wide, startlingly blue eyes.

'Hey, chill, Harry,' I said. I meant to mock him lightly, but the words came out real harsh.

Harry sat back, his expression part embarrassed, part annoyed.

'That's what you can do?' he said. 'Fall backwards off fences?'

I swallowed. 'I can protect myself from any physical harm,' I said. 'Provided I can see the danger coming – or know exactly where it is. And provided it isn't too big, like a really powerful bomb. Then I can't stop it – at least I haven't so far, though I'm working on it.'

Jeez, now I felt like a six-year-old, talking his ear off.

'Right.' Harry got to his feet. 'Let's get going, then.'

We walked in silence for a moment. It was the middle of the night, but there was still a steady stream of cars along

Euston Road. I asked Harry about his life. He told me more about his parents and where they worked abroad and how he'd snuck out of his boarding school to find me. It still felt a bit awkward between us, but at least he smiled at me a couple of times.

Don't ask me why this mattered.

As we reached the station, Harry asked if I had any idea where the code might be and I started thinking about that again. Was it written down somewhere among the possessions I'd inherited from Mom and Dad? Suddenly I felt Ed push into my mind.

Dylan? His thought-speech was urgent. *Where are you?*

What? Why? I stopped walking. Beside me I could sense Harry turn and gaze around the station concourse, but I couldn't have turned to look at him even if I'd wanted to. Ed's mind-reading is a powerful thing. Impossible to tear yourself away from unless he lets you go.

Ketty just woke me. She's had a vision of Geri demanding to know where you are. She's not sure when it's going to happen, but she thinks sometime in the morning. You need to get back here fast.

I'm gonna catch a train. The first one goes at 5.30 or so.

That's not for another hour. Ed sounded like he was freaking out.

There's nothing I can do. Cover for me, will you? Say I've gone for an early morning walk or something.

'Dylan, would you like a cup of tea or coffee? There's an all-night café over there,' Harry's voice interjected.

Who's that? Ed asked.

I could feel him start to poke around my thoughts.

Get out of my head.

Fine. Just get back as soon as you can. With a thought-spoken grumble, Ed's presence vanished.

I turned to Harry. He was staring at me.

My stomach cartwheeled.

'What were you doing just then?' he said. 'Your eyes were really focused, but it was like you couldn't see.' He sucked in his breath. 'Were you communicating telepathically with someone?'

'Er, yeah,' I said, feeling awkward. 'It's one of the others with the Medusa gene . . . they, er, he . . . he can, er, mind-read.'

'Impressive,' Harry said. 'Are you and he . . . you know?' He gazed at me intently.

'Me and Ed?' I made a face. 'No way.'

'Right.' Harry raised his eyebrows. 'So where are you going now? Are you going back to this Ed and the others with the Medusa gene? Are you all staying with the head person . . . Geri Paterson?'

'What's with all the questions?' I snapped. 'You studying for an exam on my life?'

'No.' Harry frowned. 'You know you're *really* rude. I saved your ass back there.'

My breath caught in my throat. Harry wasn't the first person to tell me I was rude, but this was definitely the first time I minded hearing it.

I shrugged. 'You were real annoying.'

Harry gazed at me a moment longer. 'Fine,' he said. 'No questions.' He fished a piece of paper out of his pocket. 'I've written my phone number on this,' he said. 'In case you find the Medusa gene code and want to talk to my dad about it.'

I took the paper, torn between relief that he was giving me his number and a slightly sick feeling that he was about to go.

'Thanks.' I smiled.

Harry's face lit up – a great, beaming smile that made his eyes crinkle. Here, in the station's bright artifical light, I could see that the irises were very pale, ringed with a darker blue . . . almost indigo. He glanced at the train announcement board.

'Your platform's up,' he said.

'You'd better piss off, then,' I said.

Harry's grin deepened. 'See you later, Red. And watch out for Milton and McKenna.'

I walked across the concourse to my train. All the way I wanted to look back to see if he was watching me. But I forced myself not to.

As I sank into my seat on the train, I felt my body relax. *Jeez*, how come I'd been so tense? Thank goodness that was over. Now I could concentrate on working out where this code was.

I thought about it for most of the journey home . . . trying to make sense of what I'd heard. According to Harry, Milton and McKenna had murdered my dad and were now after me. They already, clearly, had my phone number. It was obviously them sending the texts, though I wasn't sure whether they were trying to put me off investigating my dad's death or trying to stop me from finding the Medusa code. It surely wouldn't be too long before they tracked me down. Maybe the only reason they hadn't attacked the cottage already was because Jez and Alex and Geri were all there.

My heart beat faster at the thought. I knew I should tell Geri what I'd found out, but if Geri knew I somehow had the code, then she would want it, too. And I didn't trust her with it. I mean, I didn't think she was about to sell it as a weapon or anything, but she would definitely pass it on to the government agents she reported to. And then who knew how it would be used?

No, I had to rely on myself – and maybe the rest of the Medusa team. Yes, the more I thought about it, the more it made sense to include them. I knew now that their families hadn't had anything to do with my parents' deaths. And their skills could all be useful. When the other scientists came for me, I wanted to be as ready as possible.

Ready to take my revenge.

I fell asleep about halfway home, and woke with a start as we reached my station. The sun was fully up now. As I scrambled off the train and into a taxi, I wondered if Harry had snuck back into his boarding school yet.

I started picturing his face . . . those piercing eyes with the indigo rings.

With a jolt, I realised the taxi had actually passed the closest point in the woods to the cottage. I stopped the taxi driver, paid and raced through the trees.

It was nearly 9 a.m. now and as I approached the cottage, I could see Geri pacing about outside. Ketty stood beside her, in her usual uniform of grungy sweats and trainers.

'Where is she?' Geri demanded.

'I told you,' Ketty said, her mouth set in a determined line. 'She's gone for a walk.'

Jeez, were they talking about me?

I crept closer, smoothing out my hair. I dumped my bag behind a tree. I could come back for it later and my 'walk' would look more convincing if I didn't have anything with me.

'I asked you to tell me when Dylan was out of the shower,' Geri snapped.

'I told you, I didn't see her come out of the shower,' Ketty said. 'She'd already left when I went upstairs.'

'Ketty was with me.' Nico appeared at the cottage front door. 'What's the problem, anyway, Geri? Dylan can't get lost and the worst she'll meet on a walk are a few squirrels.'

'That's if she *is* on a walk.' Geri peered into the trees. 'She's the last person I'd expect to be communing with nature – especially this early in the day.'

'Actually, I'm totally into going for walks in the morning,' I said, sauntering out from behind my tree.

Geri's jaw dropped. Beside her, Ketty looked relieved,

while Nico glared at me, clearly annoyed at all the covering up they'd had to do.

Heart thumping, I brushed past them into the cottage. Never mind Geri and the others. I needed to focus on finding the Medusa code so the other scientists couldn't get it.

The only trouble was, I had no idea where to look.

9: THE MISSION

Maybe the code was written in Mom's diary.

I pulled out the box of my parents' things as soon as I got into my room. I scanned the diary, but all I could see were page after page of lunch dates and beauty appointments. My heart sank. I'd pored over these entries before and there was definitely nothing relevant to the Medusa gene among them.

Unless this *wasn't* Mum's diary at all and my dad had written the code in cryptic references to blow-drys and bikini waxes, I couldn't see how any kind of scientific information was held in here.

A minute later, Ketty, Ed and Nico barged in.

I looked up from the diary. The three of them were standing in a line in front of the shut door, arms folded. Nico dropped the bag I'd left in the woods on the floor.

'Thought you might like this back,' he said.

Irritated at being interrupted, I looked up. 'What do you want?' I said.

'How about a thank you?' Nico snapped.

'And an explanation about where you've been?' Ketty added only slightly more gently.

I rolled my eyes. 'Give me a break,' I said. 'You sound like Geri.'

'Don't frigging speak to us like that,' Nico said. 'We help you and include you and *lie* for you and you treat us like *garbage*.'

I stared at him. Of all the people I'd met since I came to England, I probably liked Nico the most. He was funny and street-smart and never acted all wimpy around me. In fact, we often made fun of each other. But recently, he'd been more distant. I'd put it down to him going out with Ketty. Suddenly I wondered if it was me . . . Harry's words went through my head. *You're really rude.* Normally, I just brushed stuff like that off. But here was Nico saying the same thing, more or less.

Was it true? Did I treat people badly?

I'd opened my mouth to snap at him . . . to tell them all to go away . . . but instead, I looked down at the bed I was sitting on. The cream quilt grew blurry.

Jeez, what was happening to me?

Ed's thought-speak pushed its way into my head. *Dylan, are you all right?*

Go away.

'She's upset,' Ed announced to the room. 'About a lot of things.'

I looked up, sniffing back my tears.

Nico and Ketty looked startled.

I looked at Ketty. 'Thanks for covering for me, Miss Grungy Sweats,' I said, my voice low and sullen. 'I really appreciate it.'

Nico laughed. 'Was that an apology?'

I shrugged. In an instant, Ketty was sitting beside me, her hand over mine.

'Please tell us what's going on,' she said. 'Ed said he thought you were going to this "Hub" place in London, but he didn't know why. And . . . and you know I can only see into a future that I'm going to be part of, so because I didn't go to London myself, I couldn't find out if you were going to be okay.'

I glanced at her. Ketty isn't like other girls. I mean, she's not interested in clothes and accessories like I am. She's real pretty, in a fresh, natural way – though she doesn't wear make-up and her hair is often tied back with string or whatever's closest to hand when she's getting up. Right now it was held off her face with a thin strip of blue cotton that looked suspiciously like it had been ripped from one of the sheets on her bed.

Ungroomed didn't come close as a description and yet there was an honesty in Ketty's eyes – and a determination – that you couldn't help but admire.

'Why would you want to see into the future to find out if I was going to be okay?' I snarled, turning my face away.

'Because . . .' Ketty sighed. 'Because I did . . . I do. And I'm not leaving until you talk to us.'

75

'You can trust us,' Ed urged from the door.

'Stop making this all so difficult, Dylan,' Nico added. 'I bet whatever it is, we can help . . .' He paused. '. . . Even if you hate the idea of letting us.'

I looked up at him, then at the others.

And then I told them. I spoke quietly, so that no one passing outside would overhear. It didn't take long. As I finished, Nico let out a low whistle.

'How can these other scientists – Milton and McWhatsit – know for sure that you've still got the code?' he said.

'I don't know, but they do. They've been sending me threatening texts, as well, though I don't know whether they're trying to stop me investigating who killed my dad or warning me off looking for the code.'

I showed Ketty. She shivered. 'Should we tell Geri?'

'No.' Nico and Ed spoke together.

I nodded. I'd thought about it more on the way home. Like I said before, I got along with Geri better than the others, but that didn't make it okay to spill everything now.

'If we tell Geri, she'll be after the code herself,' Nico said darkly. 'You know what she's like . . . does everything by the book. She'll have to pass the damn thing up the line to the government agents *she* reports to . . . The more people who know about it, the less control we have over how it's used.'

'Exactly,' I said.

'Anyway, we can look after ourselves better than she can,' Ed added.

I shot a look at him. As usual, his sandy hair was tufty and tousled and he was wearing his usual polo shirt and geeky trousers. When did he get so strong-minded? Five minutes ago I'd been calling him Chino Boy and he wouldn't stand up to anyone in authority.

'Okay,' Ketty said, hooking a stray strand of hair over her ears, 'then we need to find this code.'

'Er, well, we can make a start,' Ed said, 'but we've got the rest of our new mission to focus on, too.'

I stared at him. 'What are you talking about? What new mission?'

'The suspicious death of the boy at the care home,' Ketty explained, getting up off my bed.

I made a face. I'd forgotten all about that.

'I thought we'd already worked out that was really a murder?' I said. 'Isn't that why we went to the records office and looked at the report?'

'Yes, but we think we know who the murderer is now,' Ed said.

'I had a vision of him last night,' Ketty explained. 'A security guard called Roger Henson. I'd seen his picture in the notes Ed made.'

I stared at her. *Ed had made notes?*

'Henson works part-time at the care home. We checked him out . . . He's ex-army . . . with an interest in knives and explosives . . . in weapons generally . . . And not only did the boy at the care home die from a knife wound, but Henson's, like, best mates with the police officer who was first on the scene and filed the accidental death report . . .'

'Okay, but it sounds a bit vague,' I said. 'I mean, what did you see Henson actually doing in your vision? What makes you think he killed the care-home boy?'

'I saw the murder weapon. At least, I'm pretty sure I did,' Ketty said. 'The vision was a bit patchy . . . you know, just snatches of what's going to happen. I saw Henson asleep in bed . . . and this open box on the other side of the room. It was full of explosives – and a knife that totally meets the description of the murder weapon.'

'My guess is that the boy who died found out that Henson was planning to blow up some specific target. If we can get hold of the knife,' Ed said eagerly, 'it will connect Henson to the murder and get the whole case reopened.'

'As well as stop him blowing up whatever his target is,' Ketty added.

'So why not just get Geri to pass all that onto the police?' I said. 'I mean, why can't the cops go there and get the knife? Why does it have to be us?'

'It doesn't exactly have to be us,' Nico said. 'But it has to be you.'

'What d'you mean?'

'The box that contains the knife is primed to explode if anyone touches it. That's the other thing I saw,' Ketty explained. 'I described the way it's rigged to Geri and she checked it out. Those explosives won't blow up the whole house, but they would kill whoever's standing in front of the box. You're the only person who could possibly withstand the blast.'

'Me?' I stared at her. 'So why can't Nico just teleport the knife out of the box?'

'Because the knife is tied down,' Ketty explained. 'Anyway, that's not how it plays out.'

I paused. 'So you've already seen me there, tonight?'

'Yes,' Ketty said.

'And does the box blow up?'

Ketty frowned. 'I just saw Henson in bed, then the box . . . then you looking at the box . . . then the knife in someone's hand. They were just snatches of visions so . . . so the truth is, I don't know . . .'

'How reassuring,' I said, inwardly cursing the flakiness of Ketty's ability to see into the future. 'So when do we set off?'

'We have to leave this afternoon to make sure we're in position in time,' Ed said.

I groaned. I'd wanted to spend the rest of the day trying to work out where the code was.

'Look at it like this, Dylan,' Nico said. 'You scratch our backs on *our* mission, and we scratch your back on *your* mission.'

'Awesome,' I grunted. But as I looked at their faces, I knew that they were giving me a last chance . . . and I knew, also, that I didn't want to let them down.

'So will you help me look for the Medusa code? I've

checked out my mom's diary, but I'm sure there's nothing in it that could possibly be a code.'

'What about the inside cover?' Ed suggested.

'Yeah, maybe something's hidden . . . like a tiny piece of film . . .?' Nico said.

'That is *sooo* genius,' I said, pressing down on the inside cover of the diary. 'I can't feel anything.'

'It could be *really* small,' Ketty said.

Nodding, I grabbed my art knife and positioned the tip under the inside cover. I hesitated. This diary was one of the few things of my mom's I actually owned. And here I was, about to vandalise it.

'D'you want me to do it?' Ketty asked.

'Nah.' With a deep breath, I carefully sliced back the inside cover of the diary, making sure I made the tear as neat as I could.

There was nothing hidden there. I tried the back inside cover. Again, nothing.

Silence.

'What other things did your mum and dad leave you?' Nico said.

'Not much.' I indicated the box that I'd pulled out from my backpack. 'Most of it's my mom's jewellery . . . There's a few letters, too.'

'Let's have a look.' Nico walked forwards.

Ketty put a restraining hand on his arm. 'Dylan might not want us looking at her private things.'

I bit my lip. 'I'll check the letters,' I said. 'Maybe Ed

could go through all the other papers and you and Nico see if there's anything weird engraved on the jewellery.'

We got to work, but discovered nothing. After half an hour or so, Alex called us out for our morning training session. It was really sunny now and despite all my anxieties, I found myself enjoying the exercises we did. Nico and I were paired up to practise our respective psychic skills and we had a blast.

At the end of the session we had to go over the correct positions for mouth-to-mouth resuscitation. Nico, of course, wanted to do this with Ketty, but Alex made him work with Ed. I don't think either of them liked that much.

Ketty and I just got on with it. Harry kept slipping into my mind, distracting me. If I was honest, I wanted to find the Medusa code not just so that I could keep it away from Milton and McKenna, but so that I had a reason to contact him again. I didn't really understand why.

Back in the States – and at Fox Academy – I'd met lots of boys and most of them acted way more interested in me than Harry had.

'*Dylan*?' Ketty's voice brought me back to the present. She was lying on the ground, looking up at me, an irritated expression on her face. 'I just said your name *three* times which, if I wasn't breathing, wouldn't actually be possible.'

I bent over her again, trying to remember the mouth-to-mouth procedure Alex had just taught us. Pinch the nose, tilt the chin back to make sure the airway is clear, then make a seal with your lips over the person's mouth.

I made a half-hearted attempt to get into the right position for breathing life into Ketty's lungs. As I sat back again, trying to remember how long we were supposed to count before giving the next breath, Alex came over.

'How're you getting on, ladies?' she asked.

'Great,' Ketty said sarcastically. 'Though I hope I'm never in this position in real life. Helping other people isn't exactly Dylan's strong point.'

'Oh, bite me,' I said.

After lunch we discussed the mission to retrieve the knife Ketty was convinced Roger Henson had used in the care-home killing. Eventually, Geri was satisfied we all understood our respective roles, which left the four of us with just under an hour to continue looking for the code.

We found nothing. As we set off for Roger Henson's house, I was beginning to wonder if Harry had got it all wrong.

Maybe I didn't have the code after all.

The others laughed and chatted with Jez and Alex as we drove. Like always, I sat with Ed between the front and back seats, Nico and Ketty behind us.

As I twisted my mom's wedding ring round on my finger, my thoughts kept turning to Harry. It was weird, but the more I tried to put him out of my head, the more he seemed to force his way back in.

We reached Henson's home in plenty of time, but waited until it was nearly midnight and all the lights were off before making our move. At first I'd been tired. I hadn't got much sleep last night, but as we pulled on our latex gloves to ensure we left no fingerprints, the adrenaline took over. Now I was eager to get going, though Jez and Alex, as usual, were still chatting away. You could hear their anxiety – and that they were covering it up with jokes and encouraging pep talks.

'Don't forget to switch off your phones . . .' Jez said.

'. . . And never take unnecessary risks,' Ed and Ketty chorused.

The others seemed to enjoy this banter. Personally, it made me want to puke.

At last we left the car. Henson's house was semi-detached and made of brick – it looked like a million other UK houses. We kept to the shadows as we approached the side door, the tension rising.

A dog barked in the distance. All the earlier frivolity had totally dropped away now. I glanced at Ed. He was chewing on his lip. His anxiety set off my own nerves. I took a deep breath.

At least we'd broken into places so often we didn't need to speak. Nico looked over at Ketty, his raised eyebrows signalling that he wanted to know if the coast was going to be clear for the next few minutes. She nodded, not – to my eyes – entirely confidently, then Nico lifted his arm. He held his hand out towards the lock on the door and twisted his wrist.

The lock clicked open at once.

A bead of sweat trickled down my neck. I engaged my force field. We weren't sure if there was an alarm in the home so, as usual, I crept in first. Was there any kind of movement monitor in here? I looked around for the familiar red dot, usually positioned in the corner of the room. Nothing.

I took a quick look round. The inside of the house was as ordinary as the outside. A load of stripped pine furniture with plain grey curtains at the windows.

Ed was already inside my head, waiting for my signal. I could feel him lying low in my mind, trying not to distract me. I never liked it when he was there – it was hard to trust that he wouldn't sneak a peek at the rest of my thoughts and feelings.

I was working hard to keep my mind off Harry, but it was difficult – trying not to be aware of something kind of means it's already in your head.

There's no alarm, I thought-spoke.

Good.

I could feel Ed vanish from my mind. A second later they were all through the door. I followed Nico up the stairs. Ketty crept along beside me, her whole body tensed. I knew she was trying to stay focused on the near future, to sense any danger we might be about to run into, and that she was worried she might miss something.

I kept my force field fully primed in case of attack.

We were used to climbing stairs without making a sound. As we reached the dark landing, I turned to Ketty. So did Nico. There were three doors and it was down to Ketty to show us which one contained the box with the knife. She hesitated, then pointed to the door on the left.

Ed appeared in my head again.

You ready, Dylan?

Sure. I just hope Ketty's got all this right.

She's as certain as she can be. She just had another vision of Henson asleep in the same room as the box.

Awesome. I knew Ed would pick up on the sarcasm in my thought-speech, but I didn't care. As far as I was concerned, my life was in Ketty's hands right now.

And that wasn't a very comfortable feeling.

She's doing her best, Ed protested.

Get lost.

Ed broke the connection. The house was silent as I tiptoed to the bedroom door. Nico used his telekinesis to open it. Holding my breath, I peered inside. There was enough light from the outside of the house for me to make out Roger Henson asleep in the bed. His mouth moved as he snored softly. The duvet that covered him rose and fell in a steady rhythm. Beyond the bed stood a wardrobe and – just below the window – a chest of drawers. My eyes darted round the room again. Where was the explosives box?

I lit on an open metal container, standing on the floor a couple of metres away from the bed. From where I was standing I couldn't see inside.

Is he there, Dylan? Ed thought-spoke. *Is the box there?*

Yes. He's in bed like Ketty said. I stared at the metal box beside the bed. *And I think the explosives box is right here, too. Can't Nico just teleport the whole thing outside?*

No, it's wired up, remember? It'll blow as soon as anyone tries to move it. You have to untie the knife without disturbing anything else . . . It's easy to spot . . . six inches long with a serrated blade.

I took a step closer to the box. It was made of steel, glinting in the dim light that crept in under the curtains. Now I was nearer I could see a row of knives laid out just inside. A mass of wires lay in a jumble around each blade. My heart thudded. The box was going to blow as soon as I touched any of the knives. There was no way it wouldn't.

I took another step towards the box. Then another.

My legs shook as the full impact of my situation hammered home. What if Henson woke up before I reached the box? What if he had a gun? And if I did get to the knife we needed, would I really be able to handle the blast? A tiny splinter would be enough to blind me if my force field wasn't totally in place.

You can do it, Dylan, Ed murmured inside my head.

Go away.

I took the final step to the box. I bent down. There was the knife with the serrated edge, right in the centre. Wires were bunched around it. I reached out my hand, checking my force field was fully engaged.

My phone beeped. A text.

I froze, the force field draining away from me with the shock. I must have forgotten to turn my cell phone off.

I spun round. Henson was moving . . . waking . . . 'Who's there?'

Ed was inside my head screaming at me. *Run, Dylan, run!*

I stood, rooted to the spot, unable to move. Nico appeared at the doorway. I could feel him tugging at me, panicking, trying to teleport me towards him.

I glanced over at Henson. He'd seen me and I hadn't even touched the knife. He reached for a switch beside the bed. The box. He was going to blow up the box before I got the knife.

I darted forward, forgetting everything except that I *had* to reach the weapon we'd come here for. I thrust my hand inside the box. Reached for the long, serrated knife.

Force field, Ed yelled inside my mind. *Protect your—*

As the explosion erupted in front of me, Harry's face flashed into my head.

Then darkness.

10: MISTAKE

I was lying on something hard. My right side ached. Male voices were yelling in the distance. I opened my eyes. I could see carpet and the bottom of a door just a metre away.

Someone shook my shoulder. 'Dylan!' It was Ketty.

'*What*?' I forced my eyes open, completely disoriented. Ketty's face, unnaturally pale, loomed over mine.

'Dylan? Are you okay?'

In a rush I remembered being in Henson's bedroom and the metal box exploding.

'What happened?' I said. 'Where am I?'

'Nico teleported you downstairs after the explosion. You're in the hall of Henson's house. He and Ed are holding off Henson while I get you to the car. Can you walk?'

I struggled onto my elbows, identifying the distant yells – Nico and a man whose voice I didn't recognise. That must be Roger Henson.

'I should go and help,' I said.

'No,' Ketty insisted. 'Nico and Ed can manage.'

'Have you *seen* that, or are you just guessing?' I gasped.

'Nico can handle it,' Ketty said stubbornly.

I sat up, rubbing my head.

A loud crash came from the landing upstairs.

'Come here!' Henson was yelling.

I suddenly remembered why I'd been trying to reach inside the box.

'Did Nico get the knife?' I asked.

'*You* got it,' Ketty said. 'It was in your hand when Nico teleported you out of the room. Ed's got it now.' She shook my shoulder again. 'We have to get out of here.'

I nodded, rolling up onto my knees. I winced. 'My side hurts.'

'That's where you landed. The force of the explosion threw you onto the floor. Why didn't you keep your force field around you?'

I tried to think back. 'It *was* around me until my phone beeped. I guess I was just refocusing on it when the explosion happened, so it only partly protected me.'

Ketty bent down beside me. She pressed her fingers gently across my scalp. 'Is your head sore?'

'No.'

'Good. It didn't look like you hit your head. I think you just fainted.' She stood up, pulling me to my feet. 'Come on.'

As I steadied myself, Ketty's eyes glazed over for a second. Then she focused on me again.

'Ed says Nico is barricading Henson in his room. We should make a run for it. The boys'll be right behind us.'

More loud thuds from upstairs.

I tested my legs. I was fine. Just bruised along my side. My head was clearing, too.

'How come Henson wasn't knocked out by the blast?' I said. 'He was inside the room as well.'

'He must have ducked behind the bed,' Ketty explained, taking my arm. 'The rest of us were outside on the landing.'

I took a few careful steps. As we reached the front door, there was another thud from Henson's bedroom. We both turned towards the sound. Nico and Ed appeared with their backs towards us at the top of the stairs.

Nico had both arms stretched in front of him, as if he were trying to push something away.

Beside him stood Ed, the huge, serrated-edged knife I'd seen in the weapons box in his hand.

'Run!' Ketty cried.

I opened the front door and hurtled outside. Ketty raced ahead of me, glancing over her shoulder to make sure I was okay. I stumbled on the wet grass. She stopped.

'Go,' I said. 'I'm fine.'

We raced onto the road and along, to where our car was parked. I could just make out the back of Jez and Alex's heads in the front seats. As they saw us, the car revved up, reversing onto the road. Behind, in the distance, a door slammed. I looked round. Nico and Ed were pelting out of the house, just fifty metres or so behind.

The car stopped. Ketty flung herself at the back door. She opened it and I hurled myself in. I crawled across the seat, making room for her. As Ketty followed me inside, the car door shut and the locks clicked down.

Before I knew what was happening, the car was screeching off at top speed. I stared out the back window, where Nico and Ed were in plain sight, running flat out towards us.

'What are you doing?' I yelled. 'What about the others?'

Beside me Ketty gasped.

I looked round, my mouth open to yell again at Jez and Alex.

Except Jez and Alex weren't in the car.

Now I was up close I could see that the male driver was older than Jez, with shorter hair. His female passenger had turned and was facing me. She was older, too, with a jowly face and sallow skin.

Fear surged through me.

Ketty reached for the locked door, grappling hopelessly to try and open it.

'Let us out,' she yelled.

The sallow-skinned woman kept her gaze on me. 'Hello, Dylan, it's a pleasure to meet you.'

'Who are you?' I said.

'Can't you guess?' she said. 'We're old colleagues of your father . . . William Fox.'

My eyes widened. 'Milton and McKenna?' I breathed.

The woman nodded. 'I'm Dr McKenna,' she said.

My mind went instantly back to my conversation with Harry. Milton and McKenna were the scientists after the

Medusa code. The people who, Harry claimed, must have killed my dad.

My blood iced up. I stared at Dr McKenna, my heart pumping furiously as the car shot down the road at top speed.

'What do you want?' Ketty's voice rose frantically.

Dr McKenna threw her a dismissive look. 'Please don't be alarmed, Keturah, we don't want to hurt any of you. It's Dylan we're interested in.'

Beside me, Ketty's eyes glazed slightly. I guessed that Ed was contacting her through remote telepathy. Hoping Dr McKenna wouldn't notice, I took a deep breath.

'I don't know where the Medusa code is,' I said.

'That's right.' Dr Milton spoke for the first time. His voice was harsh and hoarse. 'You don't know,' he said. 'But we do.'

11: MILTON AND MCKENNA

'You're wrong,' I said to Dr Milton. 'You can't know where the code is, because I don't have it. Seriously, I have no freakin' idea where it is.'

'Where are you taking us?' Ketty interrupted. 'What did you do with Jez and Alex?'

'Jez and Alex are fine. We left them tied up on the side of the road.' Dr McKenna smoothed a strand of her long, dark hair off her face. 'Dylan, you have the code with you right now.'

I shook my head. 'I *sooo* don't have it.'

'What makes you think that she does?' Ketty insisted.

Dr Milton leaned across and muttered something in McKenna's ear. McKenna nodded.

'We'll stop in a minute,' McKenna said to us, as if that was an answer.

I pushed against the door, but it was locked. I sat back, trying frantically to work out how Ketty and I could escape. We were driving through open, deserted countryside. Even if we could get away from the car, I couldn't see how we could hope to outrun it.

Still, we had to try.

Ketty's eyes had glazed over again. She was either trying for a vision or communicating telepathically with Ed.

I slipped my hand into my pocket and reached for my mobile. I wasn't sure who I could call or how it would help, but I had to do something.

I'd programmed Harry's number in earlier. Maybe I could contact him? After all, Ed and Nico would undoubtedly have let Geri know what was happening, which would put the police on our tail. But Harry – and his scientist dad – might have specific advice for dealing with Milton and McKenna.

The car sped along. McKenna was still watching me. Ketty folded her arms.

'Where are you taking us?' she said. 'Geri will find us, you know.'

McKenna shifted her gaze from me to Ketty.

'We won't need you for long,' she said.

What did that mean?

Unnerved, I pulled my cell phone out of my pocket, hiding it in my hand. The text that had arrived while I was in Henson's bedroom was registering on the screen.

I warned u, bitch. Stop looking or die.

Another message with the sender's name blocked.

Before I could scroll to Harry's number, McKenna caught me.

'I'll take that,' she snarled. She held out her hand for my phone.

Reluctantly, I handed it over.

'I know you killed my dad,' I said. 'Whatever happens now I won't forget that.'

McKenna frowned as she reached for Ketty's cell phone, too.

'What are you talking about?' she said. 'Of course we didn't kill your father.'

'Yeah, you did. And you sent me the texts, too,' I said. 'Warning me off looking into his death and tracking down the Medusa code. They didn't work . . . as you can see.'

'I don't know what you're talking about.' McKenna glanced down, reading the text. 'We didn't send this or any other texts.'

'You're denying it?' I said.

Dr McKenna rolled her eyes. 'Why would we send you any texts like this? It doesn't make sense for us to warn you. For a start, we didn't know you were even aware of the Medusa code . . . Plus, why put you on your guard when we're waiting outside to capture you as you left the house?'

This was true. It didn't make sense, but before I could think about it any more, Dr Milton turned off the main road and drove the car slowly down a rough dirt track.

We bumped our way over earth and stones. The only

light was coming from the car's headlamps. I had no idea where we were. Milton drove us into a large wooden shed that loomed out of the darkness. He stopped the car.

We were inside some kind of workshop, with building tools lined up on the shelves and a long workbench against the wall. Beside me, Ketty glazed over again. Hoping she was communicating our position to Ed, I tried to keep the two doctors' focus on me.

'Okay, so where the hell do you think this Medusa code is?' I said.

'It's inside something you wear all the time,' Milton said. 'Show me your hands.'

'For Pete's sake!' I held my arms out towards the front seat.

'There.' McKenna grasped my right hand. Her skin was cold and rough. She clutched at Mom's white-gold wedding ring on my middle finger.

'Don't touch th—'

I was too late. In a single, swift movement she'd tugged the ring off my finger.

I stared at it, desperate to get it back. 'How can the Medusa code be on that?' I said.

Ignoring me, Milton took the ring, then unlocked the car and got out. McKenna produced a gun and motioned Ketty and me outside, too.

Milton had gone straight to the workbench. It was a trestle table, strewn with tools – everything from hammers and screwdrivers to more drill bits. Milton laid my ring on the table and switched on a powerful table lamp.

Aware of McKenna's gun, still trained on our heads, I took a deep breath. I couldn't hope to reach the ring without leaving Ketty exposed, but somehow I had to get it back off Milton.

'Why do you think that ring contains the code?' I said. 'It doesn't even have any special engraving on it, just my parents' initials and the date of their marriage. I've looked.'

'Your father *said* it was there,' Dr Milton said. 'We recently found a note, scribbled to your mother, about the code being *"inside the most precious expression of our love"*.'

Ketty breathed out slowly. 'Their wedding ring,' she said.

'Exactly,' McKenna said.

I shot a look at Ketty, hoping that she'd been communicating with Ed . . . that help was on its way . . .

Milton had picked up a tiny drill. He switched it on and a low hum filled the garage.

I watched, open-mouthed, as he positioned the drill over the ring.

'You're not cutting it open!' My voice sounded as hollow as I felt. My mother's wedding ring . . . not just the most precious expression of my parents' love for each other, but the most precious memento from either of them that was still in my possession.

'Has to be done, Dylan,' Dr McKenna said briskly. 'By

the way, I understand your Medusa gift allows you to withstand physical pain, is that correct?'

I nodded blankly, only barely noticing what she was
saying.

Across the room, Dr Milton switched on the drill. It
filled the workshop with a loud hum. In a single, swift
motion, Milton sliced the ring into two pieces.

My hand flew to my mouth. My eyes could hardly take
in what I was seeing.

Milton held one of the pieces of ring under the light.

'Dylan?' McKenna said sharply. 'I want to know more
about your Medusa gift.'

'Leave her alone.' Ketty stepped in.

McKenna raised her eyebrows. 'Perhaps we'll start with
you, Ketty. Tell me about your precognition.'

I was dimly aware of Ketty refusing to explain the limits
of her own psychic ability, but I kept my focus on Milton
and the ring.

After a couple of minutes, he turned towards McKenna,
an expression of bewilderment on his face.

'It's not here,' Milton said. He held out the ring in his
hand. It was now cut up into several tiny segments.

I stared at it, feeling sick.

'It *must* be,' McKenna said.

As she took a step closer, the huge garage doors behind
us sprang open.

I spun round. Nico, Ed, Alex and Jez were in the doorway.
With a roar, Nico teleported a ladder propped up by the door

into the air. Seconds later the ladder was hurtling over our car, straight at Milton and McKenna. The ladder slammed into them, forcing them both against the wall behind.

Pieces of ring fell from Milton's hand. With another yell, Nico forced the ladder harder against the two scientists. As they stumbled backwards, he twisted his hand in the air and all hell broke loose.

Tools and boxes and bits of wood soared into the air. A tornado of nails whirled around the garage. Beside me, Ketty darted over to the car. She crouched behind it, shielding her head.

Instinctively, I summoned my force field. I stared at Nico. He looked as furious as I'd ever seen him. Red-faced, eyes bulging, he ran towards Milton and McKenna, hurling the storm of teleported items towards them.

Jez and Alex rushed over to Ketty, still crouching behind the car.

'Get her out of here!' Jez yelled at Alex. 'I'll deal with Nico.'

But Ketty had frozen. Like me, she seemed transfixed by Nico's outburst. He was still forcing the ladder he'd teleported across the garage against the two scientists. Nails and drill bits and pieces of wood were slamming into the wall behind them. Both Milton and McKenna were shrieking their heads off, struggling to get free, but Nico held them pinned against the wall.

The ladder had fixed Milton at chest level. Head ducked to avoid all the implements rushing by, he was trying to push the ladder away. McKenna, on the other hand, was trapped at the neck, the ladder pressing against her windpipe. She was gasping, clearly struggling to breathe.

Work tools soared around their heads: a drill, a sander, a whole case of screwdrivers . . . stray items careered out of orbit, narrowly missing the car and Jez, Alex, Ketty and me.

'Stop, Nico!' Ketty yelled, banging on the car roof. 'Stop!'

Nico didn't even seem to hear her.

'Do something, Dylan!' Ketty shouted. 'He's out of control, he's going to kill them.'

She was right. Nico's rage had taken over . . . he looked insane . . .

And then I saw the hammer hurtling towards me.

It was coming. Closer and closer. About to smash into my face.

12: HIDDEN

No time to think.

Force field fully engaged, I reached up and deflected the hammer away with my fist.

I ran to Nico and grabbed his shoulder.

'Enough!' I yelled in his ear. 'Enough!'

Like a light switching off, the telekinesis stopped. All the objects in the air fell to the ground. Nico slumped, arms at his side, as if he were suddenly exhausted. In a single, swift movement, Ketty raced over and flung her arms around him.

He pressed his face into her hair. As Jez and Alex moved in on Milton and McKenna, I caught Nico's agonised whisper.

'I thought they would kill you, babe,' he said. 'I knew they were after Dylan and I thought they would kill you before I got here.'

He hugged her tighter as she whispered something I couldn't hear in his ear.

I looked away.

Jez and Alex put handcuffs on the two scientists and led them out of the garage. I went over to the workbench where Milton had been dissecting my parents' ring. Nothing remained: it had all been swept up in the tornado of Nico's telekinesis. A metallic glint on the floor caught my eye. I bent down. It was a fraction of the ring. Solid white gold with my dad's initials visible on one side: *WF*.

'Do you think we can put it together again?' It was Ed. I hadn't noticed him come up beside me.

I shook my head. 'They cut it into too many pieces.'

'I'm sorry,' Ed said.

'It doesn't matter.' I said the words, but they weren't true. It did matter. I'd lost my mother's wedding ring. It was irreplaceable.

I suddenly felt desperately, horribly alone.

I glanced at Ed. He offered a rueful, sympathetic smile.

His sympathy was the last thing I wanted.

'I don't want Geri to know they were after the code,' I said. 'She'll be all over my parents' stuff, looking for it herself.'

Ed grimaced. 'Geri already knows,' he said. 'I mind-read everything that was happening to you guys from Ketty. I told Jez, then Jez phoned Geri and told her.'

'What?' I made a face. 'Why did you do that?'

'I was trying to help,' Ed said.

I groaned, looking over at the garage door where Jez had his gun trained on Milton and McKenna. Alex stood slightly to one side, speaking to someone on her phone.

'She's calling the police,' Ed said. 'Alex and Jez had a rough time of it, too, you know. Those scientists took them by surprise, tied them up and left them in the bushes. We only found them because Jez was thrashing about, making such a noise. They were beside themselves with worry about you.'

'Whatever.' I still felt irritated that Ed had been so quick to reveal everything to Geri. Okay, I could see he was just being efficient, but it sucked, big-time, that Geri now knew there was another copy of the Medusa gene code.

'The police are on their way.' Alex came over. She handed Ketty and me our phones back. 'Jez is going to stay here with Milton and McKenna until the police arrive. I'm taking you four back home.'

As she checked out the car, Nico and Ketty walked up. Nico's face was unnaturally pale and there were dark rings under his eyes. He kept his arm across Ketty's shoulders, holding onto her as if scared to let her go. Ketty gazed up at him, her golden-brown eyes full of affection.

Nico gripped my arm. 'Thanks for stopping me.'

'Yes, thank you,' Ketty added, turning to me with a smile.

I shrugged, feeling awkward. I knew I should really be apologising for screwing everything up in Henson's house. Jez *always* told us to switch off our cell phones before a mission. It was totally my fault that I'd forgotten.

But the words stuck in my throat.

One of the car windows had been smashed in the

103

telekinetic whirlwind Nico had created earlier. Alex taped a plastic bag across the broken glass, then the five of us got into the car and drove off.

I fell into an uneasy sleep about halfway home. When I woke, we were zooming along a deserted motorway. Ed sensed me moving and looked round. I suddenly remembered seeing him with that ugly, serrated knife from the weapons box in Roger Henson's bedroom.

'Do you still have the knife from Henson's house?' I asked Ed.

'Yeah, I gave it to Jez. It's enough to connect Henson to the murder,' he said. 'We've done everything we can on that mission. It's up to the police now.'

'That's good.'

My mind went back to Milton and McKenna. They'd been so sure the Medusa code was in Mom's wedding ring. And yet it hadn't been.

So where was it?

I tried to work out where on earth it could be, but the image of the ring cut up in pieces kept creeping into my mind and I stayed awake the rest of the way back to the Lake District.

As soon as we arrived at the cottage, Alex, Nico, Ed and Ketty went up to bed, but I wandered outside to the back yard. Geri found me a few minutes later.

'Dylan, are you all right? What a terrible ordeal you've been through, dear.' I sensed she was genuinely concerned, but at the same time eager for information. 'And why didn't you tell me about the texts those scientists were sending you?' she went on in a horrified, slightly scolding tone.

I sighed. 'Milton and McKenna said they didn't send the texts.'

'Ah,' Geri said. 'Do you think they were telling the truth?'

'I guess.' I paused. 'Did . . . do you know them?'

'No.' Geri shook her head vigorously. 'But your dad was very secretive about his work. I didn't know any of his colleagues by name.'

I nodded. A cold breeze rustled the trees behind us. I went to twist Mom's wedding ring round my finger, then remembered it was gone. Geri pulled her jacket around her more tightly. She seemed lost in thought.

'I suppose if Milton and McKenna didn't send those texts, then *more* people must know about your copy of the Medusa code, which makes finding it even more of a priority.' She paused. 'I don't want to alarm you, but I don't think you'll be safe until we know exactly where it is.'

I stared at her. A shiver snaked down my spine.

'Can you think where else the code might be hidden?' Geri went on.

I shook my head.

Geri pursed her lips. I was sure she was trying to work out how to suggest we went through my parents' possessions without upsetting me.

I couldn't bear the thought of her – of anyone – poring over Mom and Dad's things. At least not right now.

'I'm really tired,' I said. 'Maybe we could do all this in the morning?'

'Of course.' Geri smiled sympathetically. She patted my arm – a slightly awkward gesture. Geri isn't exactly the touchy-feely type. 'I'm so glad you're all right. Now get some sleep.'

I trudged upstairs, feeling slightly better. Geri wasn't the warmest person in the world, but at least she cared about me . . . about us.

I went into the bedroom I shared with Ketty and sat on my bed. Considering how little either of us had with us, the room was a mess. Ketty's clothes – a mix of tracksuits, jeans and sweaters – were dotted across the floor. Her bed was unmade from this morning, the ripped undersheet dangling from the mattress. I reached for Mom's mother-of-pearl box and opened it. There were all her things, just as before. The Tiffany diary, which I'd stuck back together, the letters and other papers, the white-gold 'Ashley' necklace, the silver bangles . . .

I picked each item up in turn. The code could be concealed in any of the pieces of jewellery. I weighed the bangles in my hand. They felt heavy . . . solid . . . like the ring . . . I couldn't believe anything was hidden inside them. I mean, how would Dad know for sure these things would end up with me? And yet I was certain that, tomorrow, Geri was going to insist everything got taken away and thoroughly examined, just to be sure.

My heart sank. Harry popped, unbidden, into my mind. I reached for my cell phone. At least I had a reason to call him now – to tell him what had happened.

As I found his number, the bedroom door opened and Ketty and Ed came in. I put down my phone. I didn't want to call Harry with an audience.

'Hi, Dylan,' Ketty yawned. 'Are you tired, too?'

'I guess.'

'Nico's already asleep.'

'It's late,' Ed said. He shuffled from foot to foot.

I glanced at the time on my phone. *Jeez*, it was past 2 a.m. I couldn't very well call Harry now. I lay back on my bed. What would I say when I did speak to him?

I thought it through. At least three sets of people appeared to know my dad had left a second copy of the Medusa code in my possession: Harry and his dad; Milton and McKenna; and whoever was sending me the threatening texts, warning me not to look for it. It seemed likely that whoever was sending the texts was also the person who killed my dad, but there was no way of knowing that for sure.

It was all so confusing.

'Dylan?' It was Ed.

I looked round. He and Ketty were both staring at me. I got the impression they'd been saying my name for a while.

'What?'

'Ketty had an idea,' Ed said. 'A way I could help you work out where the code is . . . before the authorities get involved.'

I rolled my eyes. 'If *I* don't know, I don't see how *you'll* be able to help.'

'Just listen, Dylan,' Ketty urged. 'I think it could work.'

'I don't want you messing up all my stuff,' I said. 'And there isn't any other way to find the code because – as I keep telling everyone – I have no idea where it is.'

'Actually, you probably do . . .' Ed said. 'At least the memory of your parents talking about it is probably buried somewhere in your head.'

'But I was a baby,' I said. 'I wouldn't have understood what they were saying.'

'If you sensed it was important, the memory would still probably be accessible, even if you didn't properly understand it at the time.'

I swallowed, thinking through what Ed was saying . . . what he was hinting at . . .

'Do you think you could mind-read me and *see* all that?' I asked.

'It's worth a try,' Ed said.

'Though it doesn't help us work out what to do with the code once we've got it,' Ketty added.

I felt for the phone in my hand. Harry's dad would help me work out what to do with the code. I was sure of it. He'd known all along my dad had left it with me . . . he could have come after it at any point in the past fifteen years if he'd just wanted to own the code himself. Instead, he'd only got involved when he knew I was in danger, sending Harry to warn me about Milton and McKenna.

I turned to Ed. 'Okay, you can mind-read me, but only on condition that you don't go snooping around in my head.'

'I promise.' Ed came over and sat beside me on the bed. 'The easiest way in is if you let yourself think about your parents . . . go back to the last memory you have.'

I stared at him. 'I don't have any memories.'

'Not even of your mum?' Ketty said. 'I know your dad died when you were a baby, but all our mums lived until we were at least four. I can remember a few things, can't—'

'My mom died when I was two,' I said defiantly.

'Oh.' Ketty's face reddened. 'Sorry, I didn't know.'

'It doesn't matter.' Ed put his hand on my arm. 'Just let yourself think about them. If they're at the surface of your thoughts, it's the easiest way in for me.'

I looked him in the eye. 'Go for it.'

Whoosh.

In an instant he was there, inside my head.

I kept my thoughts on the contents of my mom's little box. I could feel Ed's own thoughts curl gently around them, like a wisp of smoke around a draught.

Let's go deeper, he thought-spoke, his voice very soft. *Come with me. You can stop me whenever you want.*

Okay.

I felt the tug of his mind pulling me into my own. It was the weirdest sensation, like someone else was leading me through my own head.

We were back in time. Aunt Patrice was with me,

looking at Mom's things . . . the diary . . . the wedding ring, the bangles . . . her solemn voice. 'Your mother was in a state of terrible grief . . . it was a cry for help . . .'

All my instincts wanted to resist . . . to push Ed away, but I could also feel him holding back slightly, letting me keep some control over what we were doing.

Are you all right, Dylan? Is this okay? Ed's thought-speech was irritatingly anxious.

Peachy. Get on with it.

Ed dived in deeper, back through my childhood. Times I'd thought about my parents like my first day at school . . . drawing a picture of 'my family' based on the one photo I had of me and Mom and Dad, then Patrice sniffing disdainfully that the picture didn't show her or my uncle or Paige or Tod.

Back, back in time, to less coherent memories, of a dog barking in a park . . . the fringed edge of a tartan rug, rough against my fingers . . . Paige prodding me in the stomach . . . saying, 'You smell, Dilly . . .' And then even further back to a room I had no conscious memory of . . . but was deeply familiar to me . . . my mother's face smiling through the bars of my crib . . . and then a swirl of images, all the times and places mixed up . . . yellow curtains with a pattern of beach balls rising and falling in the breeze . . . my dad lifting me high in the air over his head . . . me squealing with delight . . . Mom's anxious voice . . . a voice I didn't remember, but recognised instantly . . . 'Be careful, Will, put her down' . . . a mobile above my head . . . a teddy bear with a torn ear . . . the sound of a car . . . my dad, huge and smelling of the outside world, holding me in his arms, offering me a bottle . . . his voice gentle as he spoke to the person next to him . . . me sucking greedily at the wonderful creamy milk as his soft Scottish accent whispered: '. . . The most precious expression of our love' . . . the smell of perfume . . . gentle hands wrapping me in a blanket . . . and then tears . . . and terror . . . a fear of something . . . the known world collapsing around me . . . Mom's face blank and pale and moaning as she rocked me . . . 'I'm sorry, baby, I'm sorry, this is too hard . . .'

My mind lurched, then shuddered. Ed was pulling me away.

I realised I didn't want to go. There were memories here I wanted . . . needed . . .

Nooo. I called out in thought-speak.

We have to go.

No.

And then *whoosh*, Ed was gone. My mind felt raw, the memories ebbing away like a dream you can't hold onto as you wake.

'No,' I moaned out loud, rocking backwards and forwards.

'Dylan?' Ed's voice beside me. His arm around my shoulders. 'I'm so sorry.'

His words and touch brought me back to the room. I opened my eyes. Ed was right next to me, his eyes filled with tears. Ketty was still standing by the bed, her mouth open in horror.

'I'm so sorry,' Ed said. 'I didn't think about how you'd see all that . . . how . . .' His voice cracked. 'How hard it would be . . . and your mum . . .' He tailed off. I knew he meant my mom's depression and the way her words about things being 'too hard' prefigured her suicide.

As I pulled away from him, I realised that tears were streaming down my face and my hands were clenched tightly into fists.

I wanted to lie to them and pretend it was fine . . . I was fine . . . even deny the suicide . . . but I couldn't. I was too full of the hurt of what I'd seen. My parents had loved me so much and all that love had been torn away from us . . . from me. Because someone murdered my father and, in the end, my mom had chosen death, too, which meant . . . which meant . . . I could hardly bear to admit it to myself . . . I wasn't enough to make her stay.

I turned my face to the wall, tears still leaking uncontrollably out of my eyes.

'It didn't work,' Ed explained dully to Ketty. 'We didn't see anything about any of those things Dylan has . . . It was just horrible to feel all that pain . . . and for nothing . . .'

As he spoke, one of the memories I'd just raked up floated to the surface of my mind again. What were my dad's exact words?

'*The most precious expression of our love.*'

Of course. It all fell into place.

112

It was unbelievable, but deep in my heart I knew it was true . . .

I turned to Ed and Ketty. 'We *did* get the answer,' I said, wiping my eyes. 'I don't have a memory of it, but that's probably because I was unconscious when he did it.'

'Did what?' Ketty said, her forehead creased with a frown.

'It's the Medusa code,' I said. 'My dad didn't leave it *for* me somewhere. He left it *in* me.'

Ed shook his head. 'I don't get it,' he said. 'What d'you mean?'

'He implanted it,' I said. 'It's not just "with" me. It's literally somewhere inside my body.'

13: A DISCOVERY

I stared at Ketty, sitting on the bed opposite. She wrinkled her nose.

'Are you sure the code is inside you?' she said. 'It doesn't sound very likely.'

'I think Dylan's right.' Ed paced across the room. 'It fits with everything we know about William Fox. He was very secretive about his work. He left all his notes with his brother – I thought it was strange that he'd made a copy . . .'

'But implanting scientific data in a baby?' Ketty said. 'That's really weird.'

'Not to my dad,' I said. 'He was a doctor, remember? He'd already implanted us with the Medusa gene.'

'How would he have stored the information?' Ketty said.

I shrugged. 'Some kind of microchip under the skin, maybe? They do that with pets.'

'And when they tag criminals, I think,' Ed said.

'How do we work out where in your body it is?' Ketty said.

'There must be a scar,' I said, examining my arms.

'Yeah, but it would be really tiny now,' Ed said. 'I mean you were only a baby when he did it, so—'

'Help me look.' I tore off my top and twisted round so they could examine my back.

Ketty pored over every centimetre of my skin while I took off my jeans and checked over my legs and Ed stood, blushing and trying not to look, in the corner.

'It's no good.' Ketty sat back after a few minutes. 'There's nothing obvious. It's hard to tell what's a real scar from, say, an old scratch or a chickenpox mark or a freckle.'

'It would show up on a scan,' Ed said.

'You mean like one of those body-scan machines?' I said.

'I think so,' Ed said. 'Anyway, it's our best bet.'

'But those machines are in hospitals,' Ketty said with a sigh. 'I don't see how we can get access to one . . . unless we tell Geri about it?'

'No,' I said. 'Not yet.'

I knew in my heart that, eventually, Geri would have to know, but I needed time to adjust to the idea that there was a piece of technology hidden under my skin before I let anyone start poking around trying to find it.

'I don't want Geri taking over,' I said, trying to explain.

Ed nodded. Again I marvelled at how much he'd changed. He used to be Geri's number one fan – a major suck-up in fact. But since Luz died and Geri hadn't cared about going after the man responsible, I guess he'd realised that the people in charge of the world don't always help the people who most need it. And he'd certainly got a lot less bothered about doing what authority figures told him.

'Okay,' Ketty said, 'so what *do* we do?'

'There's another option,' I explained. 'Harry, the boy who rescued me from the Hub . . . he warned me about Milton and McKenna. His dad was a friend of *my* dad. We could go to him.'

'How do you know you can trust him?' Ed asked.

'Harry's dad has always known my dad left a copy of the Medusa code with me and he's never come after me. I'm sure he would help. Harry gave me his . . . their number.'

As I spoke, I blushed, thinking of that moment when Harry had pressed his number into my hand and the relief I'd felt that I'd have a chance to see him again.

Ketty and Ed didn't seem to notice.

Ed just nodded. 'Call him.'

I made the call, waking a very sleepy-sounding Harry.

'Hey, Red?' I could hear the grin in his voice as he recognised mine.

'Hey yourself.' I explained everything that had happened since I last saw him. I felt a little self-conscious, what with Ketty and Ed being in the room, but once Harry had fully woken up, he sounded all businesslike, which made it easier to work out a plan.

'My dad's in London right now,' Harry said. 'I'll call him. We can come to wherever you are.'

'No,' I said, imagining the battle we'd have with Geri

if Harry and his dad turned up at the cottage. 'I'll come to you. I'll get the first train to London. I'll be able to meet you in the morning.'

'Okay.' Harry hesitated. 'Let me know what train you're on . . . I'll come to Euston for when you arrive.'

I hung up and explained the situation to the others.

'Will you cover for me again?' I asked Ketty.

'No need,' she said. 'I'm coming with you. Nico, too.'

'And me,' Ed added.

'But Geri will know what's going on if we all disappear,' I said.

'We'll leave a message,' Ed said, lowering his voice. 'We'll say it was a new mission.'

'She won't believe that,' I said.

'It doesn't matter,' Ketty said. 'By the time she finds out we're not here, we'll be well away and—'

'. . . We can keep saying that it *was* a mission,' Ed added. 'There won't be anything she can do, even if she doesn't believe us.'

'But . . .' I stared at them. 'But this is *my* thing.'

'We want to help,' Ketty said simply.

'Anyway, what happens to the Medusa code affects all of us,' Ed said.

'Okay,' I agreed reluctantly.

'The only problem is money,' Ketty said.

'That's not a problem,' I said. 'I get masses from my aunt and uncle and there hasn't exactly been much to spend it on recently.'

We talked in low voices for a little longer, making more plans. Ed checked train times on his laptop and we decided to call a cab to get us to the station in time for the first train after 6 a.m. That would give us time for a few hours' sleep, but enable us to leave the cottage before the others woke up.

In the end I couldn't sleep. I was too stressed wondering about the code and where it was – and thinking about seeing Harry again.

We left the cottage without a hitch, Nico pulling back the bolts and clicking open the locks with silent ease. I fell asleep at last on the train, waking just before we arrived in London. Ed was snoring in the corner opposite me, Ketty and Nico chatting in low voices.

I was about to see Harry.

I rushed to the disgusting train toilet to check my make-up. I was wearing jeans, boots and a leather jacket with a soft blue cap pulled over my hair. I'd thought the cap suited me – I got it from a thrift store ages ago – but now I was looking at myself in the mirror I had second thoughts. I took it off and shoved it in my backpack along with Mom's mother-of-pearl box. I'd had to bring that – and its contents – with me. I was sure if I left them in the cottage, Geri would go through them.

As we got off the train, my stomach fluttered.

'So what does this guy, Harry, look like?' Nico asked, peering towards the ticket barriers.

I shrugged. Harry's face flashed in front of my eyes.

'Can't remember really,' I lied.

Ed shot me a swift look, but said nothing.

'I saw us meeting him in a vision just now,' Ketty said. 'He looks cool.'

My palms were sweating as we came out past the barrier. It was nearly 9 a.m. and the station was busy, but I saw Harry immediately.

He *did* look cool. Simply dressed, in jeans and a really stylish jacket. He smiled as he saw me. My stomach cartwheeled. I glanced at the others, checking they hadn't noticed my reaction, then back to Harry. He had followed my gaze and was now staring open-mouthed as he realised I was with three other people.

I bit my lip. In all the rush to get here I hadn't thought to warn him I'd be bringing the others.

Seconds later we were standing face to face. He was just like I'd remembered, all high cheekbones and wide, startlingly blue eyes.

'Hi,' I said.

'Hi.' Harry's face broke into a huge grin. '*I* come to meet you and *you* bring the welcome committee . . . How're you doing?'

I shrugged, smiling back. 'Fine till I saw you.'

Harry laughed. I introduced the others, watching Harry's eyes widen as he realised he was in the presence of all four people with the Medusa gene. 'It's amazing to meet you,' he said. 'Dad's at his hotel. He's got a suite. We'll be able to get some breakfast there.'

'Great, I'm starving,' Nico said. He set off for the underground with Harry. The rest of us followed.

As we walked down to the tube, Ed's cell phone rang. He glanced at it. 'It's Geri again,' he said.

She'd rung each of us in turn, every fifteen minutes, from about 7 a.m. onwards.

As Ed switched his phone off, Ketty leaned closer to me.

'Harry's fit,' she whispered.

I shrugged. 'Is he?'

Ketty giggled. 'Don't give me that,' she said. 'I can see the way you're looking at him. *And* how he looks at you.'

I glanced at her. 'What d'you mean?'

'He likes you,' she said. 'Trust me.'

'Whatever.' I was determined not to let on that it mattered, but I could hardly stop myself from smiling and my step was light as we got on the tube.

Straight away, Harry made his way over to where I was standing. I caught Ketty's eye across the carriage.

She winked.

I looked away. I'd seen how loved-up she and Nico were together. No way did I want to be anything like that.

'It's good to see you, Red.' His eyes pierced through me. 'I kinda missed you.'

'*Kinda?*' I said.

'Thought about you a lot actually,' he went on. 'How rude you are . . . what a show off . . .'

I glanced at him; his eyes were twinkling. I opened my

120

mouth to say something rude back. I don't know what exactly . . . maybe something sarcastic about how pleased I was that putting me down helped him big himself up.

But I didn't say that. I didn't say anything at all for a moment, then my mouth opened and, in a tiny, vulnerable voice I'd never heard myself use before, I said: 'It's good to have someone to trust.'

Harry blinked. His face coloured and he looked away.

Oh no.

I'd totally given myself away with all that horrible vulnerability. Where had that even come from?

Straight away I laughed. A high, fake giggle. 'I'm only kidding,' I said.

At that moment, we arrived at our stop. Harry led everyone off the train and outside. He didn't look at me again, but kept his head down, a frown now furrowed across his brow.

What had I done?

Harry walked fast down a couple of streets. At last we arrived at his dad's hotel. Still not talking, he led us towards the elevator. The others walked inside, but Harry took my arm and held me back.

'This one's a bit crowded,' he said, even though there was plenty of room. 'Why don't you guys go on ahead. Eighth floor.'

The look of astonishment on Nico, Ketty and Ed's faces was priceless. Then the door shut and Harry pressed for another elevator.

121

'What did you do that for?' I said, shaking my arm loose from his grip.

'Wanted a private word.'

Another elevator arrived. We walked inside. Harry pressed the button for the eighth floor, then fixed me with his blue eyes. 'Just so you know . . . I really like you, Dylan,' he said. He took a step closer. 'A lot.'

We stared at each other as the elevator soared eight floors. For a second I thought Harry was going to lean his face right next to mine, but all of a sudden the doors opened. He stepped smartly out of the elevator.

The others were waiting.

'This way,' Harry said. 'Come on.'

As we followed him down the corridor, Ed hung back, drawing me towards him. 'Something's not right,' he said. 'Harry seems preoccupied. I've asked Ketty to see what's going to happen with Harry's dad, but she says all she can see is us waiting in the room. She says he's just awkward cos he likes you. Is that true?'

I turned to him. 'I don't know,' I said honestly. *I hope so*.

I didn't say the last three words, but I could see the look of understanding in Ed's eyes. And he wasn't even mind-reading me.

Jeez, my feelings were literally written on my face. Did that mean Harry could see them, too?

We arrived outside the room and Harry unlocked it with a card key.

Inside the furniture was smart and modern – all light stripes and pale wood and low lighting.

'Dad'll be here in a minute,' Harry said. He turned to Nico. 'Hey, my dad's got an amazing book on telekinesis next door.' He pointed to one of the bedrooms that led off from the suite. 'D'you want to see?'

'Sure.' Nico roused himself from the couch where he'd been sitting.

It was obvious to me he had no interest in the book. Reading isn't exactly high on Nico's list of priorities, but he clearly didn't want to seem rude. He followed Harry through the door. They disappeared from sight.

Seconds later there was a dull thud, like the sound of someone dropping a book or a shoe on the floor. Ketty and Ed glanced at each other.

'Nico?' I called. 'Harry?'

No reply.

I stood up.

'Wait.' Ketty's eyes glazed.

I knew that look – she was trying to see into the next few minutes. Ed and I watched her intently. Seconds later she shook herself, focusing on the room. And us.

'*No.*' Her face paled. 'We have to leave. Now.'

'You can't.' Harry was standing in the bedroom door. 'You haven't met my dad yet.'

'What's he doing to Nico?' Ketty shrieked.

'Who?' I stared at her bewildered, then back to Harry. 'What's going on?'

123

Harry glanced at me, his eyes defiant. 'I had to do this,' he said.

'Do *what*?' I said.

'What his father asked him, of course.' A familiar figure appeared in the doorway beside Harry. A man I knew only too well.

I stared from him, back to Harry, unable to believe my eyes.

Beside me Ed gasped. Ketty moaned.

'This is your dad?' I said to Harry. '*Him?*'

'Now, Dylan, is that any way to speak to your godfather?'

And Jack Linden stepped into the room.

14: THE SCAN

Jack Linden was Harry's father? For a second, I couldn't accept it was true. But even as I reeled from the shock, I could see the similarity in their high cheekbones, wide, blue eyes and dark hair.

Jack stood, taking us all in. He looked just as I remembered him – right down to the smart designer suit, crisp white shirt and the Ray-Ban shades in his hand.

I stared at Harry. He was avoiding my eyes, keeping his gaze on Jack.

'Take Ketty into the room with Nico,' Jack ordered, putting on his sunglasses.

Harry grabbed Ketty's arm and took her next door. I watched him leave, feeling numb.

'Are you really Harry's dad?' I said, my throat dry.

Jack smiled – that wolfish grin I remembered so well from earlier in the year. 'Yes, Dylan. Not that I've spent a lot of time with him. But that's all about to change. It's like with the Romans.'

125

'What?' I stared at him.

'Roman soldiers would often leave their boys with the mothers, then call for them once they reached a certain age . . . to train them to be men.'

'What are you talking about?'

'What are you doing with Nico and Ketty?' Ed stood beside me, his fists clenched.

'They've both been drugged, so that Nico can't perform any telekinesis and Ketty won't be able to prefigure what's going to happen in the future.' Jack smiled. 'You see how well I know and understand your gifts?' He tapped his sunglasses. 'Yours included, Ed. And don't think you can scare me with the remote mind-reading either. I know that you can only read minds at a distance when you're connecting to other people with the Medusa gene. Otherwise, it has to be face to face.'

I glanced at Ed, my mouth falling open. Was that true? One look at Ed's expression suggested it was. Why hadn't Ed said anything?

Harry reappeared from the bedroom. 'Nico and Ketty are both unconscious,' he said.

'Good.' Jack moved closer to his son, speaking in a low voice so I couldn't catch the words.

I glanced at Ed, inviting him to mind-read me.

With a *whoosh* he was inside my head.

We have to stop them, I thought-spoke instantly.

How? Ed sounded frantic. *He's completely on top of everything we can do.*

Is that true that you can't mind-read people at a distance unless they have the Medusa gene? I asked.

Yes, I think so. I've tried loads of times and apart from my sister, Amy, it hasn't worked with anyone, but she and I are related so—

Why didn't you tell me? I thought-spoke angrily.

You never asked. Look, I'm going to try contacting Amy again now. I did it a second ago, but she was asleep and I couldn't wake her.

Ed broke the connection.

I turned to face Jack. Never mind remote mind-reading. How could I use my force field to help us get away?

Jack was watching Ed curiously. Harry vanished into the bathroom and shut the door.

'What about me and Ed?' I said. 'What are you going to do with us?'

'Nothing. That is . . .' Jack drew a gun from his jacket. 'I won't hurt you if you keep still and stay quiet. Can you manage that, Ed?'

Ed nodded. I stared at the gun. My heart sank. I knew that *I* could withstand a bullet from a gun – but what about the others? I couldn't leave them at Jack's mercy.

'Mmmn.' Jack grinned again. 'I think we're better off with you unconscious, too, Ed. Come with me.' He cocked the gun.

With a final despairing glance at me, Ed followed Jack into the other room. As he disappeared from view, my chest tightened. Now I was truly alone.

127

I knew the hotel door was locked, but maybe I could alert reception to the fact that we were here.

I crept across the room to the phone. Lifted the receiver.

'Put that down,' Jack barked from the doorway.

I replaced the handset and turned to him, defiant.

'What do you want?'

'The code for the Medusa gene that's inside you, of course.' Jack crossed the room and picked up a brown canvas bag I hadn't noticed before.

'How did you find out about that? You didn't know earlier this year or you'd have looked for it, then.'

'That's true.' Jack opened the bag and drew out what looked like a cross between a laptop and a gigantic cell phone.

'What's that?' I said.

'It's how I'm going to find the code,' he said. 'It's state of the art . . . a portable scanner.'

I stared, open-mouthed, as Jack set up the scanner. Harry reappeared from the bathroom. He stood awkwardly, in the doorway. He was still avoiding my eye.

'Over here, Dylan,' Jack commanded.

'No.'

Jack smiled. 'Then I'll come to you.'

He advanced, switching on the scanner as he walked. It made a low humming noise.

I backed into the corner of the hotel room. Jack, still smiling, came closer.

I steeled myself, force field fully engaged, ready to bat

the scanner away from me. But Jack stopped, about a metre away.

'Listen, Dylan,' he said. 'I know you can stop me harming you, but Ed, Ketty and Nico are completely defenceless in the other room. I assume you won't want me to hurt *them*.' He held up his gun. It was fitted with a silencer.

Damn him. Even if I provoked him into shooting at me, no one outside the suite was going to hear.

I gritted my teeth.

'It's your choice,' Jack said smoothly.

I stared at him, defeated. There was no way I could protect all the others.

'Raise your arms away from your body.' Jack brought the scanner closer.

I released my force field. Slowly and methodically, Jack moved the scanner up my back.

'What are you going to do when you find the microchip?' I asked.

'It should be just below the skin,' Jack said. 'A touch of local anaesthetic and getting it out'll be no problem.'

I couldn't believe it. After all our attempts to keep the Medusa code away from Geri and the officials she reported to . . . and now here we were, captured by a man ten times less scrupulous than she was.

My head spun.

'So how come it took you so long to capture me?' I said, trying to sound as scathing as possible. 'Harry found me two nights ago.'

'Yes, and I *was* a little cross with him for letting you out of his sight,' Jack said lightly, passing the scanner over my shoulder. 'I'd have caught up with you myself sooner, but I was still on my way back to the country. I'd been travelling here since I found out you hacked into the murder database at the records office.'

'How did you know about that?' My mouth fell open.

'An old contact with a line into the database. He alerted me that someone had done a search on William Fox. I got another contact to check the CCTV in the street outside and there you were. I knew you'd try and find out more, and that you'd think the information on your dad's murder was stored in the Hub, so I sent Harry to find you there.'

'So you knew my dad was murdered?'

Jack shrugged. 'I know his death was classified – not the straightforward accidental death that everyone said. I don't know exactly what happened to him, though.'

Was that true? I was way past being able to tell when anyone was lying to me any more.

'Did you send me texts warning me not to look into my dad's death?'

'Of course not.' Jack glanced up. 'Why would I do that?'

Again, I had no idea if he was lying or not.

'That's funny,' I said. 'Milton and McKenna said they didn't send me any threatening texts as well. One of you must be lying.'

Jack shrugged, then moved the scanner along my right arm.

'Are you working with them?' I said, seized with a sudden idea.

'Those losers?' Jack made a face. 'I'm amazed they even managed to track you down.' He sighed. 'They hacked my emails to Harry. You see, after I found out you'd been looking into your dad's death, I went back to some of his old papers and I found this note of his – a note to your mum – saying that there was a copy inside the most precious expression of their love. Milton and McKenna took that literally . . . They thought your dad meant your mum's wedding ring, which you were wearing in the photo they had of you. I knew all along William meant inside you. He adored you.' Jack chuckled. 'I told Harry not to let that cat out of the bag, though. Didn't want you finding the code before I found you.'

I glared at Harry. He gazed uneasily back, meeting my eye for the first time since Jack's arrival.

'Don't blame Harry,' Jack said cheerily. 'He was under instructions from me to do everything he did.'

'You mean, make friends with me so I'd call him if anything happened?'

'Let's get back to work.' Jack transferred the scanner to his other hand and moved it slowly along my raised left arm.

My thoughts went back to my dad's murder. Was Jack *really* ignorant about what happened? He was a low life and a conman, quite prepared to sacrifice us to make money – but he wasn't, himself, capable of murder. At least I didn't think so.

131

'But if my dad was murdered, then people at the Hub *must* have known who did it,' I insisted. 'Those government agents *own* the police. You know that.'

Jack made a face as he passed the scanner across my stomach. 'Well, I'm certain Geri didn't know anything. She was pretty senior. The only person she reported to was Bookman – the main guy at the Hub. I know your dad had a series of meetings with him just before he died, but if Bookman was the one who hushed it up, he did a very thorough job.'

I thought back to Mom's diary entries for the week before my dad was killed: *W to Hub*. Jack wasn't just confirming what I already knew – that my dad had met the head person at the Hub during his final few days. He was giving me a name too: Bookman.

My dad must have told Bookman who he suspected wanted to kill him. Which meant Bookman might know who the murderer was.

My throat tightened. 'So where's Bookman now?'

'I don't know,' Jack said. 'I don't even know his real name.' Jack frowned. 'Dammit, the scanner's not picking anything up. Let me try your head.'

'My *head*?' I said. 'My dad wouldn't have inserted a microchip into my *head*.'

'I admit it seems unlikely.' Jack moved the scanner carefully down the back of my head. 'But maybe the chip travelled. It's been there a long time.'

As he spoke, the scanner passed over the right side of the back of my neck. It let out a series of rapid beeps.

Jack froze. 'That's *it*.' He grinned. 'We found it.'

I reached my hand round to feel the back of my neck. The right side felt exactly the same as the left – muscle and tendons stretched under the skin.

'Are you sure?'

Jack nodded. 'Only problem is, it's going to be tricky to reach. I daren't take it out by myself.'

'Why?' I snapped. 'Scared you'll damage the microchip?'

'Or you.' Jack smiled.

I snorted. Like Jack cared about me.

He put down the scanner and glanced over at Harry. 'Keep an eye on Dylan for me,' he said. 'I'm going to make a call.' He disappeared into the room that already contained Ketty, Nico and Ed.

Harry wandered over to me and sat, self-consciously, on the couch opposite.

'What's he going to do with us when he gets this chip out?' I said.

'Leave the four of you in here, unconscious. He's going to up the drugs, so you'll be out for almost a day or so. By the time you come round, we'll be long gone.' Harry fixed his gaze on the table between us.

' "*We*"?' I said as viciously as I could. 'How nice for you to have such a lovely bonding experience with Daddy.'

Harry winced. 'I hadn't seen Jack in years,' he protested. 'Then he rang me and . . .'

'I get it,' I snapped. 'He's teaching you to be a man, like

133

those freakin' Roman soldiers he was talking about. Way to go, Daddy's Boy.'

'Don't tell me you wouldn't do the same, if you had a chance to spend time with your dad again.'

'My dad's *dead*,' I hissed. 'But even if he came back from the grave and offered me a million pounds, I would never sink so low as to lie and—'

'I didn't lie, not about most of it.' Harry sat forward on the couch, his bright blue eyes intent on mine. 'My birthday *is* in early February, like yours. And our parents *were* friends. Jack's your godfather, remember . . . and my mum – who *is* called Laura – was one of your dad's research assistants as well as your mum's best friend. That's how—'

'I don't care,' I snarled. 'All you thought about was yourself and impressing Daddy. You're the most selfish person I've ever met.'

There was a short pause.

'Actually, you're pretty selfish,' Harry said, clearly stung. 'I looked through my dad's notes. All the others have worked at what they can do . . . Their Medusa gift – they've developed it. But you, *no*. You have something that protects *you* and you don't care about anything else. You haven't even tried to extend that force field you create so that it protects other people.'

I stared at him, remembering what Ketty had said during our resuscitation training. *Helping others isn't exactly Dylan's strong point.*

'At least I haven't betrayed my friends,' I said with as much venom as I could muster. 'At least I'm not a coward.'

Harry stared at me, like I'd slapped him. 'I'm *not* a coward,' he said. But he sounded uncertain.

I lowered my voice, suddenly sure I'd got through to him. 'Help me,' I whispered. 'You don't have to do this. Please, help—'

'Harry!' Jack's voice was icy. He stood in the doorway of the next room, his phone in his hand. 'This is *not* what I asked you to do.'

Harry stared at the floor.

Jack turned to me. 'The doctor's on his way.'

I jumped to my feet. 'I'm not letting any doctor near me,' I said.

'May I remind you of our three hostages next door?' Jack said.

I clenched my fists. If only I'd thought to work out how to extend my force field around other people. I clutched at the back of the couch beside me, desperate to push the protective energy across the fabric. But nothing happened.

Harry was right. I had a selfish skill. And I'd only ever used it in a selfish way. Nico had said exactly the same thing, just a few days ago during that training session in the woods. And in the garage last night it hadn't even occurred to me to try and protect Ketty and Jez and Alex as they crouched, helpless, in the midst of Nico's telekinetic rage.

'I'm hungry,' Jack said. 'I'm going to order room service. Burger, Harry?'

Harry shook his head. 'What about Dylan?' he said.

'Better not risk food in case the doctor decides she needs a general anaesthetic.' Jack turned to me. 'Don't worry, that's not very likely.'

'Awesome,' I said.

Jack picked up the phone on the desk next to the window and ordered a club sandwich and a beer.

After a moment, Harry walked to the bathroom. He stopped for a second at the door, his fingers resting on the handle. Then he looked over his shoulder at me.

I'm sorry, he mouthed.

So what? I mouthed back.

I was *sooo* furious at him . . . at Jack . . . at myself . . .

I turned, angrily, and stared at the blank screen of the hotel TV. A moment later I heard the door shut.

Jack put the phone down and grinned. 'Food's on the way.'

'When will the doctor be here?' I asked.

Jack shrugged. 'Half an hour or so.'

I sank back into my couch. How could everything have gone so wrong so fast? An hour ago I'd been on the run, with my friends, looking forward to seeing Harry and meeting his dad – the one person I thought believed in *my* dad – so that I could protect the Medusa gene code from falling into the wrong hands.

And now I was a prisoner, my friends were unconscious and the Medusa code was about to be taken and sold and used for who knew what terrible purpose.

Worst of all, Harry had betrayed me. He'd looked into my eyes and lied and, like a total idiot, I'd trusted him. His *I'm sorry* meant nothing. He didn't care about me at all.

I closed my eyes.

I didn't feel numb any longer.

For a moment I didn't even feel angry.

I hurt.

I shook myself. I wasn't going to let Harry and Jack beat me. Somehow I had to find a way out of here – with the others *and* the Medusa code.

15: THE MICROCHIP

It was nearly midday before the doctor arrived. He was a slight, elderly man with greying hair and a stoop. His name, or so he said, was Dr Mims. He didn't look me in the eyes as he passed the scanner back and forth over my neck, then directed Jack, Harry and me into an empty bedroom.

I lay face down on the bed, fuming. Every cell of my body wanted to resist . . . to protect myself with my force field . . . but Jack's threat that he would hurt the others if I didn't co-operate rang in my ears.

Somehow I *had* to find a way out of this that didn't leave Ed and Nico and Ketty at Jack's mercy.

Dr Mims applied an anaesthetic cream to the back of my neck.

'That'll just need a few minutes to take effect,' he said.

I looked around. *Think, Dylan, think.* My heart pounded.

Jack checked his watch, then pulled a bottle of pills from his pocket. He tipped three into his hand and handed them to Harry.

'Go and top up the others,' he said. 'Just one pill under the tongue. I don't want to take any chances.'

As Harry left the room, Jack spoke in a low voice to Dr Mims.

I felt the back of my neck. The patch of skin where Dr Mims had applied the anaesthetic cream was numb. Any minute now the two men were going to come over and Dr Mims would take his scalpel and cut through to the microchip.

I couldn't let it happen.

I looked around the room for a weapon.

My eyes lit on the glass bottle of mineral water on the table by the bed. I could smash that and use it to keep both men at bay while I escaped from this room. It had its own lock, which meant I'd even be able to keep them contained afterwards.

That would just leave Harry. Hopefully, I'd be able to deal with him, too. Even if I couldn't take the others with me, at least I could get down to the hotel lobby and raise the alarm.

I shuffled towards the bottle of water, but instantly Jack was at my side.

'It's time,' he said.

Dr Mims hovered over me, scalpel poised in his hand.

Instinctively, I tensed, ready to use my force field. Then I let the energy field dissipate. It was better to let Dr Mims remove the microchip first. Afterwards, he and Jack would be focused on that, not me, which would give me a better chance of taking them by surprise.

'Don't move,' Dr Mims warned.

I lay rigid, feeling the sharp blade tingle against my skin. There was no pain.

The room fell silent. Then Jack gasped.

'There it is.' Dr Mims' voice rose in triumph above my head. 'Perfectly intact.'

'Amazing,' Jack breathed. 'Let me see it in the light.'

Face down on the bed, I couldn't feel, or see, what they were looking at.

Dr Mims bent over me again. 'No need for a stitch,' he said. 'The cut was tiny. There's hardly any blood.'

I heard the ripping sound of a plaster being torn away from its backing, then felt the doctor's fingers pressing on my neck.

As he turned away from me, I rolled off the bed and grabbed the water bottle.

Wham. I smashed it against the bedside table. Water splashed out, over the floor, down my leg. Dr Mims jumped back.

I glared at Jack. He was across the room, by the window. His eyes widened in horror as I brandished the bottle.

I rushed towards him. He drew his gun, silencer attached. Dr Mims shrank back against the wall.

Jack pointed his gun at me. The tiny microchip lay on the window sill at his side, a black dot on a piece of white card.

'No.' Jack's voice was resolute. He pointed the gun at me.

I braced myself. My force field should hold against a single bullet.

I reached for the microchip. Jack pointed the gun at my head. His hands were shaking.

'Stop, Dylan.'

Keeping my eyes on him, I fumbled for the microchip. There. I snatched it up.

'No.' Jack frowned, like he was trying to force himself to pull the trigger.

'Harry!' he yelled.

He lowered the gun so it was aiming at my knee. I suddenly knew he wouldn't shoot to kill.

My instincts had been right. Jack, for all his many faults, was incapable of cold-blooded murder.

Microchip clutched in my hand, I backed towards the door. Dr Mims was now cowering against the wall on the other side of the room.

'Stop or I'll shoot,' Jack said.

'Go right ahead.' I steeled myself, force field still fully primed.

Jack pulled the trigger. The bullet exploded out of the gun. I held my breath, feeling it tap lightly against my shin, then fall to the ground.

Triumphant, I hurled the broken bottle at Jack.

As he ducked, the glass smashed against the wall. I darted outside the room, fumbling for the key.

It was a flimsy lock. Jack would break it down in seconds. That's if he didn't shoot his way out.

I didn't have much time.

I hurtled across the room, force field primed. With a roar, I pushed open the door to the other bedroom. Surely Harry had heard the shot and the yells . . .? I was ready for whatever he threw at me.

He was bent over Ed. I couldn't see Nico or Ketty.

'Get away from him,' I shouted.

Harry glanced up, his eyes full of alarm. Ed was blinking, rubbing his sandy hair.

'It's okay, Dylan.' Nico appeared from the other side of the room, Ketty at his side. 'Harry's helping us. He gave us something to bring us round.'

I stared at Harry. He looked back at me, an expression of shame and defiance in his eyes.

'About time,' I snarled.

A loud thump sounded from the other side of the suite.

'Jack's gonna break that door down any second,' I said. 'We need to get out of here.'

'Come on.' Harry helped Ed to his feet.

The five of us fled towards the suite door.

Another huge thump. The door rattled on its hinges.

'Have you got the Medusa gene code, Dylan?' Ketty grabbed my arm.

'Here.' I opened my fist. The microchip nestled, still on its white card, in my palm.

Harry and Ed reached the suite door. They sped out, into the hotel corridor. Ketty raced after them.

With a violent crack, Jack's door flew open. Red-faced, Jack appeared in the doorway. He raised his gun and pointed it at Nico.

Harry's words about me being selfish flashed into my head. I concentrated on willing my force field – still surrounding me – to cover Nico, too.

It didn't work.

Nico teleported the table by the window into the air. With a yell, he slammed it against Jack.

Jack stumbled. Fell. Behind him Dr Mims shrank back, his face white.

Nico grabbed my arm and we flew down the corridor after the others.

Harry, Ketty and Ed were at the elevator. Harry pressed the button frantically. As Nico and I speeded up, the door opened. We all bundled inside.

Ketty pressed for the ground floor.

A sudden silence descended. My heart pumped through it, drowning out my thoughts. I could feel Harry's gaze on my face, but I didn't look at him.

The elevator door opened and the five of us hurtled out and across the hotel lobby. We ran at full speed, following Nico down a series of streets.

After a few minutes, Nico stopped. We stood panting.

Ketty recovered first. 'Where now?' she said.

'Where's the microchip, Dylan?' Ed asked anxiously.

'Here.' I felt for the tiny dot again. How could something this small contain so much powerful information? 'But I don't think we should go to Geri until we've worked out what we want to do with it.'

The others nodded.

'That means going to the cops is out, too,' Nico said. 'If we go to the police, we'll be back with Geri, Jez and Alex in hours.'

Harry cleared his throat. 'I have a suggestion,' he said.

'Why should we listen to you?' I said.

'He did help us escape,' Ketty said.

'I didn't realise . . .' Harry paused.

'Didn't realise what?' I snorted. 'What Jack was going to do? Don't make me laugh.'

Harry shook his head. 'I didn't realise how it was going to feel betraying your trust.' He fixed his eyes on me and it was like the rest of the world and the traffic around us and Nico, Ketty and Ed vanished. 'I didn't realise how bad I was going to feel.'

We stared at each other.

'So what's your suggestion, Harry?' Nico said impatiently.

Harry looked round at the others. 'Jack's my dad, okay, but he and my mum split up ages ago. We hadn't seen him for years. Mum has no idea he's been in touch with me.'

'So?' I said.

'My mum's a scientist. She worked for William Fox,' Harry went on. 'And she cares about all of you, especially Dylan . . . She was best friends with her mum. She'll know what to do with the microchip.'

'That's your suggestion?' I said with contempt. 'Give

144

me one good reason why we should trust you to take us to your mom when going to your dad ended in—?'

'Ed?' Ketty said.

Ed focused on Harry's eyes. A moment later they glazed over.

A few, long seconds passed, then Ed broke the connection.

'He's telling the truth,' Ed said simply.

I wondered if Ed had seen any reference to me in Harry's thoughts. But no way was I asking. Instead, I just gave a loud, angry sniff.

'Fine,' I said. 'Where does Mommy live?'

'We can't go to their house,' Nico said. 'Jack's bound to think of looking there.'

This was true. And obvious.

I blushed at not having thought of it.

Harry fished out his phone. 'I'll call her,' he said.

A moment later we had a meeting place and time. The Science and Art of Medicine Gallery at the Science Museum in half an hour.

As we set off, Harry glanced at me again. I looked away. Too many feelings were swirling in my head. I didn't know what to make of any of them.

All I knew was, we could easily be running from a bad situation to a worse one.

And, once again, we were in Harry's hands.

16: LAURA'S SECRET

Nico peered into the glass case. He pointed to a set of small iron instruments. 'What on earth are they?' he said.

'Doctors used them a few hundred years ago,' Ed said. He was standing by the plaque next to the case. 'This museum is fascinating. I haven't been here for ages. I'd forgotten how good it was.'

Nico rolled his eyes. 'You are *such* a geek.'

'Why shouldn't I be interested in history?' Ed sounded mildly annoyed.

Nico laughed and said something back, but I wasn't paying real good attention. I was all focused on the museum gallery doors.

Partly, I was scared that Jack had followed us, though I couldn't see how he could possibly know where we were.

Mostly, I was consumed with curiosity – and apprehension – waiting for Harry's mom . . . supposedly my mom's best friend. Harry himself stood beside me, looking out for her, too.

It wasn't that crowded in the room – a large school party had just left – and we could see the doors in and out from where we were standing.

I wasn't just anxious about trusting Harry's mom with the Medusa code. It was also her connection to me. She had known both my parents well . . . she'd known *me* as a baby . . . I didn't often meet people who fell into that category.

'There she is.' Harry scooted off towards a slim, elegant-looking woman in jeans and a cream shirt with a highlighted blonde ponytail.

Ed, Nico, Ketty and I watched as Harry spoke quietly to his mother. She was clearly angry at him and agitated, glancing over at us as he talked. Her gaze shifted from person to person, finally settling on me. Smiling at last, she motioned to Harry to stop talking and walked away from him, towards us, with her arm outstretched.

'Dylan?' she said. 'Oh my God . . . oh my . . . I'm Laura.' Her voice cracked as she spoke. To my consternation, her eyes filled with tears.

'Er . . . hi,' I said, feeling awkward.

'I'm sorry.' Laura brushed away the tears impatiently. 'It's just you look so like your mother. Ashley was one of my closest friends. There's not a day goes past when I don't think about her. I can't believe the danger Harry's just put you in.'

I shrugged, not knowing what to say.

Laura turned to the others. 'This is overwhelming,' she said. 'I worked with William Fox for many years and though he never shared the details of his work on the Medusa gene with me, I understood enough about what he was trying to do to know that the four of you are . . . well, if half of what he predicted worked out, then you're nothing short of a miracle.'

'Mum?' Harry's face pinked with embarrassment. 'Maybe we could talk about this all later. It's just that Jack will try to follow us and we need to do something to—'

'I think you've done enough, Harry,' Laura said sharply.

'You said you would help with the microchip,' Nico ventured.

'Of course.' Laura smiled. 'I will. I'll do anything to help. Especially you, Dylan. For your mother's sake. And your dad's. Will you trust me to do that?'

I looked into her pale blue eyes. They radiated warmth and sincerity. And yet, after my dealings with Harry, there was no way I could take her on trust.

I looked away. 'Ed needs to check her out,' I said in a low voice.

'What, so we assume everyone's guilty until I prove them innocent?' Ed shook his head. 'That's not right.'

Laura gazed at us bewildered. 'What—?'

'Not right, but necessary,' Nico interrupted. 'Go on, Ed. You mind-read Harry.'

'Harry was different. I had to see he wasn't lying again,' Ed persisted, his face reddening, 'but I don't feel comfortable mind-reading people who haven't done us any harm and who we don't have any reason to suspect.'

'You can really read people's minds?' Laura's eyes widened.

'We suspect *everyone*,' I snapped. 'That's our baseline.' I clenched my fists.

'Normally, I'd agree with Ed,' Ketty butted in, her voice calm and soothing. 'But under the circumstances I think Dylan is right and checking that Laura is telling the truth is justified.' She turned to Laura. 'We apologise in advance, but Harry brought us to you and—'

'It's fine.' Laura swallowed. She glanced at me, then looked away quickly. 'I can understand why you want to do this. Go ahead, Ed.'

Reluctantly, Ed met her eyes.

A few seconds later he broke the connection. 'I didn't go deep,' he muttered. 'But she genuinely wants to help us.' He turned to me, his voice all smug and vindicated. 'And she *really* cares about you . . . so there.'

A confusion of emotions swirled inside me. Embarrassment. Irritation at Ed. Relief we could trust Laura. And hope.

I turned to Laura, trying to sound practical and serious.

'What do you think we should do?' I said.

'My car's parked on a meter, round the corner,' Laura said. 'I'm planning on driving to our holiday home in Sussex. It's very out of the way. I only bought it last year. Jack doesn't know about it, so it's completely safe.'

I glanced at Nico and Ketty. I wasn't quite so convinced that any house was as safe as all that. Various experiences

149

had taught me that determined people with good resources can track you down wherever you are. Still, it took time to do the tracking. And, right now, Laura was our best bet.

'Going with you seems like the smartest option,' I said.

The others nodded.

The holiday home was cute. Much prettier than the cottage in the Lake District, with flowers sprawling across the front yard and sleek wooden blinds at every window. It was modern, made from glass and reclaimed wood, and full of state-of-the-art devices such as solar-powered heating and movement sensors to control lighting and water. Ed was transfixed, wandering from room to room completely fascinated. Harry seemed happy to show him round. I sensed he was glad to get away from his mom for a bit. Nico and Ketty disappeared as soon as Laura had offered everyone a drink.

Which left the two of us. Laura had already told everyone she wanted to talk to me privately before examining the contents of the microchip. She hadn't even asked to see it yet. I kept feeling for it in my pocket, palms breaking into a sweat as I remembered Dr Mims' fingers on my neck earlier.

We sat down in the small room that clearly served as an office. It was more cluttered than the rest of the house, with a long wall of bookshelves groaning with an amazing variety of fiction and non-fiction. I was scanning the titles when Laura, who'd been making coffee, came in with two steaming mugs.

She set them down on the low table beside the armchair in the corner and motioned me to sit there as she drew up another chair.

I did as she asked, suddenly feeling nervous.

'I want to reassure you that as far as I'm concerned, the Medusa gene code is yours to use – or destroy – as you wish.' Laura paused. 'You have so little of your father's and, though I'm sure the government who paid for the research would disagree, this is *your* inheritance, Dylan. It doesn't belong to anyone else.'

Laura's pale eyes glinted as she spoke. She waited a second, perhaps to see if I was going to say anything, then she cleared her throat. 'Do you have any questions for me . . . about your parents or . . . or anything else?'

My head was just about spinning off with questions. I hesitated, trying to work out which I wanted to ask first.

'How did you know them . . . my mom and dad?' I said.

'I knew your mum first, of course, then, later, I got a job working as one of your dad's research assistants. He was . . .'

'I know,' I interrupted, not wanting to hear the list of my dad's failings again. 'He was a difficult man . . . stubborn, secretive, paranoid . . .'

Laura frowned. 'Actually, I don't think he was any of those things until he realised the Medusa gene he'd discovered – and was so proud of – was going to kill the wife he absolutely adored. Well . . .' she continued, 'he *was* always rather secretive and very particular about his work, but he

151

had to be. He was working at such a high level. You know he was a genius, don't you, Dylan?'

I looked away. I'd been told this before and I'd never really known what to make of it.

'Well, he wasn't just a genius. He was a passionate man, with a strong sense of justice. And he was a good boss, too. I was very fond of him.'

'What about Mom? How did you meet her? When? Where?'

Laura's frown deepened. 'Did your Aunt Patrice not tell you anything?'

I shook my head. 'I never heard of you,' I said. 'I mean, I didn't know about Jack before he turned up and no one ever mentioned you – or Harry.'

Laura sighed. 'I met your mother at university. She was doing a junior year abroad, majoring in drama, and I was in my last year studying biochemistry. Chalk and cheese, we were. Ashley was the life and soul of every party. There was a song out at the time about two friends . . . how one was serious and the other "let the air in". That was me and her. A couple of years later she was over on a visit and I introduced her to William. He was quite a bit older, of course, but they fell in love like nothing you've ever seen. Besotted with each other, they were. Ashley was my best friend. That's why they made Jack and I your godparents.'

My mouth fell open. I'd known about Jack, but . . . 'You're my *godmother*?'

Laura nodded. 'When Ashley passed away, I begged the courts to let me have you, but she'd died without leaving a will and her sister took precedence. Patrice was married and wealthy and a blood relation. Whereas I . . . well, Jack was flaky, to say the least . . . I was basically a single mum living on a research assistant's salary. I'd only just got another job after William dying and your mother's death hit me hard, too. I probably sounded deranged when I kept insisting I could look after you as your mum would have wanted. I think the lawyers thought I was after your money, but I wasn't. I just wanted what was best for you.'

'Aunt Patrice was *sooo* the one after my money,' I said bitterly.

Laura shot me a keen look. 'She wouldn't let me see you, Dylan. I tried to visit, I sent presents and photos, but Patrice returned them all. I attempted to take her to court over that as well. I argued you had a right to see me. I was your godmother. But you were in America and the lawyers were very expensive, and when I went out to see you, she actually threatened to call the police if I didn't leave . . .' She tailed off, tears in her eyes.

I put my hand on hers. 'At least we've met now,' I said. 'Even though it is . . . like this.'

Laura wiped her eyes. 'I could throttle Harry for putting you through what just happened. Honestly, he—'

'Jack's very persuasive,' I said, suddenly feeling defensive of Harry. 'And he is Harry's dad.'

'I know.' Laura sighed. 'He hadn't been in contact for

153

over three years then, according to Harry, he showed up a week or so ago, promising Harry the earth . . . flashing his money about. I had no idea . . .'

She talked on for a few minutes, describing how, years ago, she'd fallen for Jack herself. Then she rummaged in a cupboard and fished out some pictures. One christening picture – dated the July after I'd been born – struck me in particular. I was wearing a long, white gown. For once, my face wasn't red-raw with eczema. In fact, I looked cute. Mom was holding me, beaming, with Dad on one side and Jack and Laura on the other. An older baby with a shock of dark hair was wriggling in Jack's arms. That must be Harry. Behind my dad stood a solemn – and very young-looking – Fergus. He was talking to a heavily pregnant lady with long, dark hair. That had to be Nico's mom.

'You can keep it if you like. Show Nico,' Laura suggested.

'Thanks.' I took the picture. 'It's hard . . . Mom looks so happy here . . . It's hard to believe what she . . . what happened . . . I mean, it was less that two years afterwards . . .'

I glanced at Laura, hoping she knew what I was talking about. As I did, a terrible anger flared inside me. If Laura really had been Mom's friend, how come she hadn't known Mom was close to suicide? How come she hadn't done anything to stop her?

Laura met my gaze without flinching. Then she leaned forward in her chair.

'Thank you for bringing up . . . what happened to your

154

mother, Dylan,' she said, clearly making some effort to keep her voice steady. 'I wasn't sure how to tell you, but I'm just going to come straight out with it. Two things actually. They're going to be a bit of a shock . . .'

'What?'

'Well, in the first place, your dad was murdered,' she said. 'It wasn't an accidental death.'

'I know that already,' I said sharply. 'I saw his file. It was in the murder section – and classified. Not that anyone else believes it.'

'Your mum believed it. She investigated what happened. She was convinced William had been killed deliberately.'

My heart pounded. This was exactly what Aunt Patrice had said.

'Who did she think killed him?'

'She didn't know his real name. She referred to him as Bookman.'

Bookman. Jack had mentioned him earlier. Bookman was in charge of the Hub . . . the person my dad had gone to see several times in the week before he died.

'That's not all,' Laura went on. 'The night she died, your mother called me. She said she was frightened that Bookman knew about her suspicions . . . that he was going to come after her. We agreed to meet two hours later. I was going to put the two of you on a flight to somewhere remote. But your mum never turned up.'

I stared at her. 'What are you saying?'

'I'm saying that it wasn't just your dad who was killed, Dylan. I don't have any proof, but I'm one hundred per cent sure your mother didn't commit suicide.' Laura squeezed my hand. 'Your mother was murdered, too.'

17: REVENGE

Harry knocked on the door, calling his mother away.

Laura apologised for leaving me, but to be honest, I was glad to have a moment to sit and let what she'd told me sink in.

According to Laura, *both* my parents had been murdered. And not by rival scientists trying to get hold of the code for the Medusa gene, but by Bookman – the boss of the Hub – the man with overall responsibility for the original Medusa gene development project.

A dead weight settled in my guts as the revelation hit home. Everything I'd been told before about my mom was wrong.

She hadn't been hysterical or paranoid.

She'd been right.

The cup of coffee Laura had brought me earlier grew cold in my hands. It was hard to accept what she'd told me, but it made sense. Bookman was the very person Dad kept going to see in his last few days. A person he'd confided in . . . and trusted. Mom had known Bookman had betrayed him . . . killed him . . . but she had no one to turn to . . . no one who could help her. And she paid the ultimate price for that.

A terrible fury swept through me. I could barely keep still.

Two lives taken. A baby left orphaned.

How *dare* anyone commit such crimes? It was almost beyond comprehension.

Footsteps sounded across the hall outside. A light knock on the door, then Ketty poked her head round.

Her golden-brown eyes were anxious. 'Hey,' she said. 'Laura told us what she just told you . . . She's coming back in a sec, but I just wanted to check you were okay.'

'I'm fine,' I lied.

Ketty nodded, then hesitated for a second.

I turned my face away. I didn't want or need her pity. Or the others feeling sorry for me.

No. I only wanted one thing. Revenge.

I had to find Bookman and make him pay for what he'd done to my mom and dad. For what he'd done to me.

The door clicked shut as Ketty slipped away. Moments later Laura reappeared. She was flushed and flustered, full of apologies for leaving me on my own.

'We can talk about it some more later,' she said. 'Right now I think I should take a look at that microchip your dad left you.'

158

Jeez. I'd almost forgotten about the microchip. I fished it out of my pocket and handed it over silently.

At Laura's urging I followed her into the living room, where her laptop was set up on a polished wooden table. The others were all in there. Their low chatter stopped as we walked in.

Great. They'd obviously been talking about me – probably Laura's dramatic revelation about my mom's death.

I didn't look at them, but seconds later felt Ed's mind pushing into mine.

Are you okay, Dylan? he thought-spoke.

Go away.

Ed broke the connection.

I bit my lip. I knew I was being rude, but I didn't really care. I hated them all knowing about my private stuff.

Hated it.

I hung back as Laura took a machine that looked like a miniature scanner out of a nearby cupboard, then sat at her computer.

'We use these to decode microfiles. This is an old chip, but the decoder should still work on it,' she said, plugging it in and carefully laying the microchip inside it.

'Man, it's *tiny*,' Nico breathed.

Laura nodded. 'Yes, William would probably have been able to inject it with a hypodermic needle.' She closed the lid of the scanner, then pressed a series of keys on her computer. 'It'll take a moment to get past the data encryption, but I know the system William used. It won't be a problem.'

Long seconds passed. Everyone stared at the screen. Everyone except Harry.

I could feel his eyes on me, but I didn't look up. I stayed where I was in the doorway. After a moment, a line of numbers and symbols flashed up on the screen.

'There.' Laura sounded both relieved and triumphant. 'William really was amazing to have thought of doing this.'

'Is that it?' Ketty said. 'The code for the Medusa gene?'

Laura peered at the screen. She scrolled carefully down the page, her lips moving as she read the hieroglyphics. 'As far as I can understand it, yes, this is it.' She reached the bottom of the screen, where the numbers and symbols stopped and several lines of text took their place. I was too far away to see what they said. The others crowded round, blocking the screen from my view.

Laura turned round. 'It's a message for you, Dylan. From your dad.'

The others backed away as I approached the computer. There at the bottom of the page was the only direct communication I'd ever had from my father.

My most precious daughter, darling Dylan. By now you will know what I have left in your care. If I am no longer alive or able to tell you these things myself, please forgive me for imposing this responsibility on you and know that wherever you are and whoever you have become I trust that you will use what I am giving you wisely. As it stands,

it brings both great power and great tragedy. Remember
that and know you have all my love,

forever. Daddy x

I read the message twice, so lost in what it said I didn't
even hear Laura speak until she touched my arm.

'Dylan?' Her voice was gentle.

I turned to her, forgetting everyone else standing around.

'What did he want me to do with the Medusa code?'
I said.

Laura shook her head. 'I don't know. I don't think he
would have kept it at all if he wanted it destroyed. But I'm
certain he wouldn't want it to be used if it still kills the
mothers of the babies implanted with the gene.'

A thought leaped into my head. 'Could you work on it?'
I said. 'Could you amend it so that it didn't kill the moms?'

Laura shook her head. 'I wish I could say yes, but I
simply don't have the knowledge or skill required.'

Ketty made a small movement beside me and I was
suddenly aware of everyone else in the room.

'I think we should destroy it,' Nico said.

'But the science behind it is revolutionary,' Ed protested.
'If someone could just work out how to make it work
without killing anyone, then—'

'But how can you ever guarantee *how* people will use
it?' Ketty interrupted. 'I mean, I agree with Ed that it's
wrong to destroy such a great scientific achievement. But
Nico's right, too. We can't let it fall into the wrong hands.'

161

'What do you think we should do, Dylan?' That was Harry.

Again, I could feel his eyes on me, but I didn't look up.

'I don't know,' I said. 'I need time to think.'

'And everyone needs something to eat.' Laura closed the lid of her computer and switched off the scanner. She drew the microchip out and handed it over to me. 'This is yours, Dylan. I'm going to rustle up some soup and pasta. Maybe the rest of you could help?'

I took the tiny black dot and stared at it as the others followed Laura out of the room. My head reeled with options. I had no idea what I should do with the microchip.

There was a bookshelf to the left of the desk. I reached for a random book.

The Tao of Physics.

It seemed as good a place as any to hide the chip. I opened the book at page 99 and laid the microchip inside. Replacing the book, I went back to the desk and sank into the chair.

My thoughts went back to my parents' murder. At least now I knew the truth . . . that it *was* murder. For a moment I felt a huge sense of relief. My mom hadn't wanted to leave me. She'd loved my dad and me. She *hadn't* wanted to die.

And yet she had been killed in cold blood. The fury rose inside me again. If my mom had been right, then Bookman, the man in charge of the Hub, was the murderer. If I wanted revenge, my next step was to find him.

I opened Laura's laptop. She hadn't closed anything down. The whole machine was totally available to me. Glancing round to make sure I was still alone, I searched for Bookman's name in the documents files.

Nothing.

'What are you doing?' Harry spoke from the doorway.

I slammed the laptop lid down and spun to face him. 'None of your business,' I said.

'I came to ask whether you wanted chicken or tomato soup,' Harry said suspiciously. 'Why were you looking at Mum's computer?'

'I was just messing around,' I said. 'I wasn't looking at anything in particular.'

'You're lying.' Harry fixed me with his piercing blue eyes.

I stared back, my throat suddenly dry. 'You're in no position to lecture me about lying,' I said.

'Fair enough.' Harry kept his gaze on me. 'But don't lie to my mum. She doesn't deserve that.'

He was right. Not that I was going to give him the satisfaction of saying so. Instead, I got up and walked past him, across the hallway and into the kitchen. It was brightly lit, with stainless-steel appliances and a wooden block in the centre of the room. Laura stood over the stove, a pan in her hand. Ketty and Nico were chopping stuff on the counter; Ed was rummaging in a cupboard.

They all looked up as I entered.

'How do I find Bookman?' I asked Laura.

She blinked. 'What . . . er, why?'

'I need to know the truth about what happened to my parents. According to you, Bookman is the prime suspect. Where does he live?'

'I don't know.' Laura's mouth fell open. 'But even if I did, I couldn't let you go after him. It's too dangerous.'

I marched over to the stove where she stood. The ring on the near left glowed red-hot.

'Look,' I said. Summoning my energy field I pressed my hand onto the stove top. I could feel its warmth, but the burning heat couldn't touch me.

Laura gasped. 'Don't . . .'

I lifted my hand and held it out to her, palm up. 'See?' I said. 'Not a mark. I can look after myself. And I'm going to find Bookman whether you help me or not.'

The tension in the room rose.

Laura nodded slowly. 'I'm not lying to you, Dylan. I don't know where Bookman lives or even if he's still alive. I never met him. Your mum never met him, either – and your dad never mentioned him directly to me.'

'Geri would know,' Ketty said breathlessly.

'I don't think we should involve Geri until we've decided what to do about the Medusa code,' Ed said.

I shook my head. 'I disagree. Geri's our best lead to Bookman. Anyway, what we do with the code is *my* decision.'

'Don't we get a say, Dylan?' Nico asked, a touch of annoyance creeping into his voice.

I said nothing, but a plan was forming in my head.

'No, of course we don't,' Nico went on angrily. 'Man, when are you going to start realising we're all in this together?'

I looked up, my gaze shifting from him to Ketty to Ed. 'Actually, I do realise that.' I hesitated, knowing I had to say the words, but finding it hard to face up to what they meant. I took a deep breath. 'I've got a plan for getting the truth out of Bookman, but I'm going to need all your help to make it happen. Are you in?'

18: THE HACKER

I called Geri from my cell phone. She answered right away, her voice curt.

'Where are you, Dylan? What on earth are you all doing?'

'We're on a mission, Geri,' I said.

'I thought I'd made it clear you were to do *nothing* without a full briefing from me so that I can provide you with proper back-up,' Geri said, speaking at a hundred miles an hour in a low, terse voice. 'It's bad enough the four of you picking your own missions without you clearing off in the middle of the night to carry out some secret—'

'Listen, Geri,' I interrupted. 'I didn't call to fight with you. We need to find someone and I think you know where he lives.'

'Who?' she said suspiciously.

'This guy . . . Bookman. He used to run the Hub – he was your boss years ago. Remember?'

A long pause.

'Of course I remember. Why do you want to find Bookman?' She hesitated. 'Does this have something to do with the Medusa gene code?'

'Sort of,' I said. 'I think Bookman knows who killed my dad. In fact, I think he might be the one who did it.'

Geri sucked in her breath. 'Dylan, I'm sorry, but that's nonsense. Your father died in a traffic accident.'

'I've got reason to believe he was murdered by Bookman,' I said.

'What reason?' Geri gave an exasperated sigh. 'Dylan, this would be funny if it wasn't so stupid. I worked for Bookman. He was a . . . a civil servant . . . a man behind a desk shuffling papers and rubber-stamping agency operations.'

'My mom thought it was him. She confronted him and he killed her to stop her talking to anyone else.'

'Your mother was an hysteric. She went to pieces after your dad died. Where are you getting this ridiculous information?'

I said nothing. I didn't want to mention Laura – or Harry. I was sure Geri would be able to find us once she had Laura as a lead.

'Dylan, think about what you're saying. *Why* would Bookman want to kill your dad? It doesn't make sense. William Fox was a genius. He was *working* for us. Yes, he'd gone off the rails a bit since he found out the Medusa gene killed the mothers, but we were all confident he would calm down. It wasn't his fault that the gene mutated – he'd tested it *and* the virus it was embedded in. After he'd got over the shock, he would have come back to work. *That's* what Bookman wanted. William Fox back in the lab. Not William Fox dead.'

'Maybe my dad knew something bad Bookman had done,' I said stubbornly. 'Maybe Bookman thought he had a reason to kill him.'

'*What* reason? It wasn't in Bookman's interests to kill him – we were both trying to encourage him to resume his research. We didn't want the mothers to die either. We'd already agreed that we wouldn't use the Medusa gene code until William had sorted out the problem – and clearly, we *didn't* use it, otherwise there'd be more than just the four of you.'

I paused. It was true that there were only four of us with the Medusa gene. Ed had even admitted earlier that he was only able to do remote telepathy with Nico, Ketty and me. Everything Geri said made sense and fitted in with everything I'd ever heard about my dad . . . until I saw his death listed as murder.

I took a deep breath. 'I saw the classified report on my dad's death when we did that mission to the records office, looking into the accidental death at the care home.'

'*What?*' Geri sounded utterly shocked.

'My dad wasn't filed under accidental death. He was filed under murder.'

'No,' Geri insisted. 'You weren't reading it properly.

That database covers murders *and* classified deaths. I've seen it. Your dad's death was in the classified section because he was doing secret work for the government. That's standard practice.'

I hesitated. Was that true? I couldn't remember what the precise name of the database had been.

It didn't matter. My mom had been sure Bookman had killed my dad. I owed it to her to at least discover if that was true.

'I'm going to find Bookman whether you like it or not. I have to at least *ask* him what he talked to my dad about in those meetings they had.'

'No, Dylan. This has to stop. You must—'

'I've got the Medusa gene code,' I said. 'I found it in my mom's things. You can have it if you tell me where to find Bookman.'

I waited, heart in mouth, certain that offering up the code would weigh more heavily with Geri than any other argument. Not that I had any intention of handing it over to her.

Still, I'd cross that bridge later.

There was a long silence. 'I don't know where Bookman is,' Geri said eventually. 'I haven't worked for him for many years. He retired soon after the Hub closed down.'

'You can find anyone, Geri,' I said. 'We both know that. You're probably tracking this call right now, so you can find us.'

'I don't have those kind of resources up here.' Geri sighed. 'Fine, I'll get back to you – but it'll take time.'

'Make it soon,' I said, 'or I destroy the Medusa code. It's the last remaining copy, remember?'

'I'm putting in a call to the MoD right now.' She hung up.

I hurried back to the others, drew Nico, Ketty and Ed to one side and told them what Geri had said.

'She's buying herself time,' I said. 'And I don't trust her not to try and track us through our phones, whatever she says. We need to dump them and be ready to move as soon as she calls back with the info on Bookman.'

'Er . . . don't you think this is all moving a bit fast?' Ed said.

'Only for someone who moves like a snail,' I snapped.

There was an awkward silence.

'Come on, Dylan. You have to admit Ed has a point,' Nico said. 'Geri does, too . . . I mean, Bookman didn't have much of a motive for killing your dad, did he?'

I shrugged. 'I still have to find out why my mom suspected him.'

'I don't trust Geri with the Medusa code,' Ed said sullenly. 'I don't want you to give it to her.'

'I'm not going to,' I said. 'That was just bait. For Pete's sake, Ed . . . Geri isn't the problem. She might be ambitious and manipulative, but her number one priority has always been to protect us. Let's stay focused on finding Bookman.'

We sat in silence for a while longer.

At last Geri called back.

'I can't access the information immediately, Dylan,' she said. 'I've put in an urgent request at the MoD for them to examine the archives, but they're saying it'll take a while to come through. The best thing you can do for now is come home. We can make a plan for dealing with Bookman together.'

'I'll think about it.' I hung up, switched off my phone and turned to the others.

'Geri didn't take the bait,' I said, feeling annoyed. 'She says she's pushing the MoD to give her information on Bookman, but I don't know . . . it all sounds real slow.'

'Er, Dylan?' Harry was standing in the doorway leading back to the little office. He looked slightly self-conscious. 'Can I have a word?'

I caught Ketty's eye as I stood up. She winked at me.

I threw her a disdainful look. After the way Harry had made a fool of us earlier, he stood no chance with me whatsoever. Not that he ever had.

I stalked over to where he was standing, aware that the others were watching us.

'What?' I snapped.

'Come in here,' Harry said in a low voice.

I followed him into the office. 'What's this about?' I said.

He stared at me, then shut the door that separated us from the others. For a second I thought he was going to try and kiss me. I steeled myself, force field firmly engaged.

Harry took a step towards me, then stopped. 'I think I can trace Bookman,' he said.

I wasn't expecting that.

'How?' I said.

'He worked for the government . . . for the MoD. There's a list of employees and former employees . . . names, addresses, dates of birth . . . basic stuff.'

'And you have access to this list?' I said.

Harry's face reddened. 'Not exactly, but I know how to hack into it.'

I stared at him. 'How?'

'My dad showed me,' he said. 'It was on one of his random visits. About three years ago. Please don't tell Mum. She doesn't know, but he taught me loads of basic hacking stuff. It's kind of a hobby of mine now. I don't do anything dangerous or bad with it, and I'm not that good, but government stuff's relatively easy.'

I raised my eyebrows. 'You're full of surprises, aren't you?'

Harry kept his gaze on me. In the dim light of the office his pupils were huge, making his eyes a much darker blue than before.

'Go on, then,' I said. 'See what you can find.'

Without speaking, Harry pulled a laptop from the backpack he'd been carrying earlier, and sat with it open in front of him. I let him work for a few minutes, watching as a stray lock of hair fell over his eyes. He was concentrating intently, his forehead furrowed in a frown.

'There,' he said at last. 'Bookman – no longer on active service. Real name: Gordon Jellicoe. Last known address: Benton Manor, Benton. He's seventy-two.'

I leaned over his shoulder, looking at the screen. A picture of a man with glasses and greying hair met my eyes. He looked like a typical, middle-aged office worker. I frowned, remembering Geri's description of Bookman as 'a man behind a desk shuffling papers'. Was this man really capable of murder?

Harry turned towards me. Our faces were suddenly very close.

I pulled away abruptly.

'I'm getting the others,' I said. 'We're going to Bookman's house now.'

'What about me?' Harry jumped up.

'You should go home with your mom.'

'I want to come with you,' Harry insisted. 'I could be useful.'

'How?' I sneered. 'What's *your* superpower? A bit of hacking and lying doesn't cut it with us.'

I walked out, not looking back at him. I told the others what Harry had found and that I was going after Bookman whether they liked it or not.

'Fine,' Nico said. 'But we take things one step at a time.'

'Whatever.'

'What are you four discussing?' Laura said, walking out of the kitchen.

'Geri called back with Bookman's address,' I lied, not

173

wanting to get Harry into trouble. 'We're going to go there now. You and Harry should leave here, too. I don't trust Geri not to try and track us down.'

'But you can't go after Bookman on your own,' Laura protested. 'It's dangerous.'

'We're going anyway,' I said.

'At least let me drive you,' Laura said. 'You'll get there faster.'

I glanced at Nico. He nodded.

'Okay, thanks,' I said. 'But you and Harry have to wait outside.'

'Of course,' Laura said.

I wasn't entirely sure she was as willing as she sounded to let us confront Bookman alone, but we could deal with that later.

We arranged to leave in five minutes. I spent the time taking a plastic bag and a trowel from the kitchen, then retrieving the microchip from *The Tao of Physics*. Making sure no one could see me, I snuck into the back garden. There was a patch of loosely dug earth near a bed of white flowers. It was hidden from view of the house by a large oak tree. I put the microchip inside Mom's mother-of-pearl box, then wrapped it in the plastic bag. I dug a shallow hole just behind the flowers, buried the box, then rushed back inside.

Everyone was ready. We clambered into Laura's car, going over the plan again. Harry said nothing. I hadn't looked at him since he'd done that hacking for me. I hoped at least he appreciated I hadn't ratted him out to his mom about it.

We stopped just long enough to ditch our mobiles and buy pay-as-you-go phones. As we drove on, the conversation died for a bit. I pulled on my headphones and listened to some music. I was trying to keep my mind off the mission, but in the end it was Harry that kept intruding into my thoughts – and how he hadn't tried to kiss me in the office after all.

19: BOOKMAN

It was totally dark by the time we arrived on the outskirts of Benton. The journey there had been a nightmare – Laura's satnav wasn't working properly and we'd missed the turning to the village three times. Ironically, once we'd reached Benton itself, the manor wasn't hard to find . . . three imposing storeys of brick set around two courtyards. There was a wide, tree-lined drive in front of the house and what appeared to be a landscaped garden behind it.

'Bookman seems to have done real well for himself,' I commented drily.

The house was mostly in darkness, but one room on the ground floor was lit. As we drove past, however, it was impossible to see in. Drapes had been drawn at the window.

Laura parked her car a short way down the road.

'I'm coming with you,' she said, opening her car door.

'No.' Nico slammed it shut using telekinesis. 'We already agreed. We're on our own here.'

Laura jerked round, clearly shocked.

'We appreciate your help,' Ketty said quickly. 'But we'll be better and faster on our own.'

'But—'

'We're not walking in the front door and asking politely for an interview,' I said. 'We have to take him by surprise . . . *force* him to talk to us.'

'How are. . . ?'

'Come on, we need to go.' Nico was already out of the car.

Jeez, and he says I'm rude.

I reached forward and patted Laura on the shoulder. 'Harry will stay with you,' I said. 'And we've got our new phones on silent. Call if you see anything suspicious. That'll be the best help you can give us.'

'And don't worry,' Ed added, reaching for the door handle. 'We'll be fine. We've done this before.'

Laura nodded reluctantly. Harry opened his mouth, presumably to protest about being left behind. I leaned forward before he had a chance and whispered in his ear.

'I'd feel so much better if you were looking after your mom,' I said. 'Please?'

He sighed. 'Okay.' He sat back.

As we walked silently to the house, the usual confusion of thoughts rushed through my head. It's always the same just before any mission – anxiety and excitement and going over the plan. But this mission mattered more. I could barely contain the volts of adrenaline shooting through me.

I *had* to find out what Bookman knew.

Suddenly Ed was in my head.

What do you want to do with Bookman if, er . . . if you find out, er . . . he did murder your parents?

Kill him. The thought leaped into my head before I could stop it. I could feel Ed's shocked reaction.

Dylan, you can't . . .

Chill, I thought-spoke. *I won't actually do it.*

Okay. Ed sounded uncertain. He broke our connection immediately. I was sure he was communicating what I'd told him to the others.

Great. Now they'd all think I was some kind of psycho.

As we crossed the drive, keeping close to the trees at the side, I tried to shake off all the other thoughts and focus purely on my force field.

Ed was in my head again.

Ketty says Bookman's in there alone, but her vision's a bit hazy . . . she's just getting a glimpse of his face.

Great.

It's not her fault. She can't be sure of what she's seeing . . .

Sounds a bit weird. Could be a trick or a trap.

That's what Nico said. He says we should lay a false trail . . . send someone in separately so we come at the house from two directions.

Sure . . . I should go in alone. I can protect myself better than anyone else.

That's what Nico said.

Well, isn't Nico full of great ideas?

178

Ed broke the connection.

We reached the end of the line of trees. From here to the house was a five-metre dash where we would be totally exposed. I strained my eyes, trying to make out any sights or sounds.

Not even a security camera. The only sign of life inside the house was that lit-up room.

I touched Nico lightly on the shoulder. 'You take the front door,' I whispered. 'I'll go in through the window.'

He nodded, then set off with Ketty and Ed. I followed close behind. The others reached the front door. They stopped, crouching in the shadows.

I raced on, my rubber soles making no sound on the tarmac drive.

I reached the room with the light on. The drapes were tightly drawn.

I glanced round at Nico. He held up three fingers.

Three. He lowered one finger. I braced myself.

Two. This was it. No second chances.

One.

I raised my fist and punched through the window. *Smash*. In an instant I was hauling myself up, hands clutching the sides of the glass. My energy field protected me from the jagged shards as I raised myself up on the sill, threw back the drape and jumped into the living room.

It was long and narrow . . . old-style, with two smart, stiff couches and an armchair at the far end of the room, turned to face a real fire burning low at the grate.

I looked around. Scratched floorboards covered with rugs. A sideboard . . . china ornaments . . . a couple of photographs.

Empty.

In the near distance I could hear the groan of the front door opening. A second later Nico, Ed and Ketty were inside the room.

For a second we all stood, silent, straining again to listen for sound.

Nothing.

'There's no one here.' I couldn't hide the disappointment in my voice. I'd been all primed to attack . . . at the very least to defend myself from danger . . .

I glanced at the photos on the sideboard again. One was a family group, the other a line of businessmen sitting in chairs. A more formal picture. I went over.

One man appeared in both photos. Middle-aged, greying – the same guy from the MoD file that Harry had hacked into.

'Are we in the right place?' Nico whispered.

'We must be.' I handed him the photo. 'This is Bookman.'

'I don't get it.' Ketty said quietly. 'I got a definite look at his face and I'm sure it was in this room. I saw the curtains.' She pointed to the dark red drapes, which hung along most of one wall.

I followed her gaze, then looked carefully around. The only part of the room not totally visible from here was the seat of the armchair facing the fireplace at the far end. I glanced at the floor beside the chair. The rug was bunched up, as if it had been pushed back in a hurry . . . the floor underneath was covered in scuff marks.

'Looks like somebody turned the chair round,' Ed whispered, his voice full of confusion. 'Can you see anything, Ketty?'

'No, I'm too stressed now,' Ketty grumbled.

I rolled my eyes.

'We should search the rest of the house.' Nico took a step towards the door.

'Wait.' I walked over to the armchair. 'We should check this out first.'

'I think if anyone was sitting in that chair, they'd have heard us by now,' Nico said impatiently.

'Just let me look.' Force field primed, so I couldn't feel the sweat that I knew was dripping down the back of my neck, I took another step closer.

Ash from the fireplace was scattered across the floor . . . a poker lay on the floor.

I stopped. A shoe was peeking out past the leg of the chair.

My heart beat fast. Someone was sitting in the chair.

I edged closer, holding my hand up to quiet – and warn – the others.

Bookman was in the chair, staring into the fireplace.

Is it him? Ed thought-spoke.

Yes.

It was definitely Bookman, albeit with whiter hair and more lines on his face.

I wasn't making much noise, but surely he should have sensed me moving into his sight line by now.

What the hell was going on?

Behind me I sensed Ketty stiffen. Was she seeing something in the future?

I took another tiny step closer. Bookman didn't even flicker, just kept staring into the fire.

'Hello?' My voice was low and hoarse.

No response.

Heart totally in my mouth, I reached forward and touched Bookman's shoulder. He fell forwards, slumping over the arm of the chair.

I jumped, barely stifling a scream. Behind me the others gasped.

I stared at the red stain on the back of the chair, then at the blood on the back of Bookman's head.

I reached forwards and touched his wrist. The skin was still warm, but the heat was fading. And there was no pulse.

'Oh my God,' Ketty whispered.

I turned to the others. Their faces were pale with shock in the dim lamplight.

'Well, we've found him,' I said, trying not to sound as shaken as I felt. 'But someone else appears to have found him first.'

'Is he . . .?' Nico started.

'Dead,' I said. 'Totally dead.'

20: THE CLUE

We stared at Bookman's body, still slumped in the armchair.

I'd only seen a dead person once before . . . that was on our last mission, when Carson, the guy who'd imprisoned us, shot Ed's Spanish girl, Luz. Ed, who had been right next to her, had naturally totally freaked. But Ketty and I had been in the room, too, witnessing everything. It was one of the most horrible moments of my life.

I looked at Ed now, wondering if he was thinking of Luz, but he was frowning, staring at the floor at Bookman's feet. I followed his gaze. A number had been roughly outlined in the ash from the fireplace.

343

'What's that?' I pointed.

Ed glanced up. 'Bookman must have written it with his shoe.'

And then a door slammed somewhere else in the house.

I jumped. So did the others.

'What was that?' Ketty hissed.

Nico raced to the door.

'I bet that's the person who killed Bookman,' I whispered.

I glanced back at the dead body and forced myself to touch Bookman's arm again. As I'd thought before, the skin was warm. He hadn't been dead long.

'Come on.' Nico beckoned me towards him. 'Just you and me.'

'But if I'm not with you both, I won't be able to see what's going to happen to you,' Ketty protested.

'I don't care,' Nico said. 'Stay with Ed. If anything happens, he can reach us telepathically.'

Ketty was clearly going to argue, but Nico had already set off along the corridor. I followed him, careful to make no sound as I ran. We reached the hallway. The front door was to our left. Stairs leading up to a carpeted first-floor landing were on our right.

The sound of footsteps echoed over our heads.

Nico put his finger to his lips, then pointed up the stairs.

I nodded to show I understood, then followed him up, my force field fully primed.

We reached the first floor without hearing or seeing anyone. We stood silently for a moment. Then a loud crash sounded from the left.

We crept towards the place the sound had come from. My heart pounded as we passed door after door. Each one was open wide as if it had just been flung back on its hinges by someone in a desperate hurry.

My mind ran over the possibilities. It couldn't be a coincidence that Bookman had been murdered just before I reached him. Someone clearly wanted to get to him before I did.

But why? There could only be one reason. They must be after the Medusa code and think, for some reason, that I believed it was here.

I went through my list of suspects. Who knew about the existence of the code? Milton and McKenna – but it couldn't be them because they were in custody. Geri – but Geri already knew the code was with me. She'd have no reason to kill Bookman anyway. Same with Jack.

Which meant there must be someone else I didn't even know about, prepared to kill to get their hands on the code – or, at least, stop me from getting it.

A shiver rushed down my spine. Running footsteps outside caught my ear.

I raced into the nearest room and looked out the window. I was just in time to see a shadowy figure darting into the trees outside.

The person was dressed in dark, shapeless clothes – I couldn't make out any details, not even if it was a man or a woman.

A second later a car engine revved.

I turned to Nico. 'Should we go after them?'

He shook his head. 'The car'll be out of sight by the time we get outside.'

I gazed round the room. I'd raced to the window so fast

I hadn't even noticed what a mess it was in . . . armchair overturned . . . clothes and duvet on the floor . . . ornaments and lamps strewn everywhere . . .

'Looks like whoever killed Bookman was looking for something,' Nico said.

'Yeah, that makes sense.' I explained my theory that the intruder was searching for the Medusa code, now certain it was right.

'Why would anyone think the code was in here, though?' Nico said. 'This is just a spare room.'

I had to agree it was strange. And it didn't explain the number – *343* – that Bookman had traced in the ash on the floor downstairs.

A moment later Ed and Ketty appeared.

'I just spoke to Harry and Laura,' Ed said. 'They're fine. They heard a car screeching off, but didn't, er, see the guy who ran out.'

'Why didn't they follow him?' Nico said.

'Harry wanted to, but Laura insisted they should stay and wait while we check everything out.' Ed paused. 'I didn't tell her about Bookman . . . when she hears, she'll want us to leave straight away.'

'Good call,' Nico said approvingly.

The four of us wandered round the room for a bit, hoping to find some clues to the identity of the mysterious intruder.

After a minute's searching, Ketty unearthed an open safe door, partially hidden by the duvet that had been torn off the bed.

The safe was empty.

'Maybe the murderer thought the code would be in there,' Ed suggested.

'Or maybe he was just an ordinary burglar who got disturbed by Bookman, killed him, then came up here to steal from the safe?' Nico said.

'So Bookman gets murdered just before we arrive,' I said. 'It's a bit of a coincidence, isn't it?'

Nico shrugged.

'I don't like thinking about that dead body downstairs,' Ketty muttered.

'Me neither,' Ed added. 'We should call the police . . . or at least Geri.'

'I'll call her.' Ketty went out into the corridor to make the call.

Nico and Ed followed. I took a last look around the spare room. That armchair falling over must have been the crash we heard. It was a heavy piece of furniture and couldn't have fallen on its side by accident. Which meant the intruder had deliberately pushed it over. But why? The safe was on the other side of the room. You didn't need to go anywhere near the armchair to reach the safe from the door. And the noise the armchair made had nearly given away the intruder's position to us.

Unless the noise was the point.

It was like the way we'd entered the house. I'd come in through the window, alone, drawing attention away from the others.

If you want to cover your tracks, lay a false trail.

Maybe the intruder hadn't been looking for either the code *or* the contents of the safe. Maybe they were trying to stop *me* finding something. Maybe all this mess was just a way of distracting my attention from what they'd really been looking into.

I stood up. What would someone want to stop me from finding?

The answer was obvious. The truth about my parents' murderer.

Mom had been convinced that Bookman was the killer. But suppose she'd been wrong? Suppose the murderer was another person entirely . . . someone from outside the Hub, maybe . . . someone who just *knew* Bookman?

That would make more sense. After all, Geri had been adamant that there was no reason for Bookman to kill my dad. It was, as she'd said, in the government's interests to have him alive . . . to coax him back to work on his Medusa gene research.

I raced outside. Ketty was still explaining what had happened to Bookman. I grabbed the phone off her.

'Geri?' I said breathlessly.

'Dylan?' Her voice was tight with impatience. 'What the hell are you doing? I *told* you I would get you Bookman's address. We could have done this together instead of you barging in and nearly getting yourselves killed—'

'Who else could have killed my dad?' I blurted out. 'Apart from Bookman, I mean?'

Geri tutted. 'For goodness' sake, dear. I've told you a million times . . . your father died in an accident. Now I absolutely insist the four of you come back here straight away. I'll send the police to pick you up.'

There was a clattering on the other end of the line. The familiar sound of Alex laying out the plates on the cottage table. 'I'm on the phone, Alex,' Geri said tersely, presumably in response to the noise.

I sighed. Clearly, Geri was going to be of no use.

'Don't send the police,' I said. 'We'll make our own way home.'

I shoved the phone back at Ketty and wandered back into the room with the open safe.

If this messed-up room was a false trail, then there must be some clue to my parents' murder elsewhere in the house.

I wandered into the corridor again. Nico was speaking to Geri, now. I could hear him saying that we would come back to the Lake District cottage as soon as we left here. As agreed, he didn't mention that Harry and Laura had been helping us. None of us wanted to get them into trouble with Geri.

Ed glanced at me as I passed, but I paid him no attention. I strode along the corridor, taking a look at each room in turn.

Jeez, they were all as neat and tidy as each other – a long series of spare rooms. Some with beds and wardrobes, others virtually empty. And this was just one corridor of a huge, three-storey house.

To search it thoroughly would be impossible. Laura and Harry wouldn't wait outside forever. And, anyway, Geri was going to have the police round to pick us up before you could say 'crime scene'.

I reached the landing.

Think, Dylan, think.

If the open safe was a red herring, then the information the intruder hadn't wanted me to see must be in a completely different room.

I thought back to the sequence of sounds we'd heard. The door slamming that prompted Nico and me to investigate had been followed within twenty seconds by the footsteps we'd heard coming from the first-floor corridor – pretty much where I was standing right now.

I looked across the landing to the corridor that led off in the opposite direction. The slamming door had come from there.

I set off at a jog, counting the seconds off under my breath.

One Mississippi

Two Mississippi

Three Mississippi

After twenty beats, I'd reached the end of the corridor and a single shut door. It was heavy – an internal fire door – and would certainly make a big noise if it was left to slam shut. My heart in my mouth, I opened it.

There was nothing special inside. Some kind of library with long rows of bookshelves built against every spare centimetre of wall. Half were covered in books, the other half laden with bulky files.

I looked around. Nothing appeared to have been disturbed.

I crossed the room and examined the bookshelves more closely. Like everything else in the house, they were neat and ordered.

Except . . . it wasn't much, but as I peered along the next row of shelves, one of the huge files was slightly behind the others. As if it had been shoved back into place in a hurry.

Palms sweating, I pulled out the file and opened it up.

It was produced by the Ministry of Defence, and huge and heavy in my hands. I laid it on the table and turned the pages. Some sort of reference file, complete with information on everything from storage facilities to spying equipment. The word *Classified* was stamped on every page. For a second I wondered what on earth Bookman was doing leaving such a thing lying around on his bookshelf, then I caught the date at the top of the page. *Jeez*. This file had been printed in the early sixties. Everything inside it must be hopelessly out of date.

I skimmed the pages. A whole chapter on hidden cameras. They looked as big as bricks . . . a far cry from today's fibre-optic technology. The next page carried a picture of a room filled with some huge machine I couldn't identify.

The caption underneath the photograph read: *State-of-the-art computer for Wardingham facility*.

That massive machine was a computer? I shook my head and turned another page. Then another.

I couldn't see why anyone would be interested in this reference file, other than as some sort of history lesson.

I turned the next page. The jagged edge of torn paper met my eyes.

I frowned. Why had this page been torn out?

I stared, intently, at the text on the bottom of the previous page.

The domestic archive will extend three hundred yards underground and will contain minutes of all meetings not considered vital to national security. Floor plans for the new archive are shown opposite. These outline room layouts, the venting system and a new state-of-the-art security system. It is hoped that . . .

The text obviously continued on the next page – the one that had been torn out.

I blinked, trying to make sense of what I'd found. Why would anyone want to tear out a page of an ancient file showing floor plans to a building built in the sixties?

'What are you doing?' Nico was in the doorway, looking cross. Ketty stood beside him.

'We have to leave,' Ketty insisted. 'We couldn't stop Laura coming inside. She's downstairs now, freaking out over Bookman's dead body. Ed's trying to calm her down, but—'

'Geri's sending some special police to deal with Bookman and escort us back to the Lake District,' Nico interrupted. 'I thought you'd want a heads-up.'

'Thanks.' I held out the MoD file, showing the torn page. 'I think I know what Bookman's murderer was after.'

Ketty took the book. 'This is ancient,' she said. 'Why would he be interested in some old MoD building in Wardingham, wherever that is?'

'I don't know, but the killer took the trouble to stop and take the page even though he knew we were in the house, so it must have meant something to him.'

'How do you know the killer tore that page out?' Nico said, in a voice that suggested he thought I was totally mad.

As I explained about the sounds we'd heard and my retracing of the intruder's footsteps, Ketty pored over the MoD file. Nico's expression remained sceptical.

'I still don't buy it,' he said.

'Well, maybe you'll buy this.' Ketty pointed to a red stain on the back cover of the file. 'It's blood and it's still wet. I'm betting it's Bookman's, wiped off the murderer's fingers.'

Nico raised his eyebrows. 'What do you want to do, Dylan?'

I met his gaze. 'I'm going to this Wardingham archive.'

'How d'you know it ever got built?' Nico protested.

'Even British builders don't take more than sixty years to build something,' I said tartly.

'Don't let Ed hear you say that,' Ketty said. 'His dad's a builder.'

'What do you think you're going to find there?' Nico went on.

'I'm going to find out the one thing I really need to know,' I said. 'I'm going to find out who killed my parents.'

21: WARDINGHAM

We got away from Bookman's house just after midnight and just before the police arrived. Laura was totally freaked out – frantic that if Bookman's murderer was still at large, we were in terrible danger.

'If he'd wanted to kill us, he'd have attacked us back in the house,' Nico pointed out.

'And remember, we have our Medusa skills,' Ketty added. 'They give us an edge over almost anyone.'

'I know,' Laura said anxiously, 'but this is still *such* a dangerous situation for you all to be in.'

'We've been in worse,' Ed said quietly. He glanced at Harry. 'I think you should take your mum home . . . lay low for a bit. We didn't mention you to Geri. No one needs to know we've seen you or that you're involved in any of this.'

Harry looked at me. I nodded.

If I was honest, I didn't want Harry to leave – but knowing that he and Laura were safe was more important.

'I have to check out the archive,' I said. 'I don't believe Bookman's murderer would have torn out that page if they hadn't really needed it. And if they're going to the Wardingham building, then I have to go, too.'

'At least let me give you all a decent meal,' Laura protested. 'Maybe a few hours' sleep as well.'

'Thanks, but we need to get going,' I said.

Laura voiced a few more objections, but she knew she was beaten. After a while, she took us to an all-night internet café in the nearest large town, where Ed did some speedy online research. Ironically, although Bookman's 1960s file spoke of the MoD building at Wardingham as a state-of-the-art new facility, the building was about to undergo major renovations.

'According to this article from a couple of months ago, there's going to be some cutbacks in staffing to pay for internal recabling work,' Ed said, peering at his screen.

'Man, there's three hundred yards of archives in that basement,' Nico read over his shoulder. 'And we have no idea what we're looking for.'

Laura went to the bathroom, as Ketty clicked on a link at the side of the page. The outside of the building appeared. It looked like a prisoner-of-war camp, surrounded by a series of high, wire fences, and an entry hut guarded by two men in army uniform.

'Can you guys really get past all that?' Harry's tone was part awed, part sceptical.

'No problem,' Nico said. 'Unless there's something we don't know about.'

For a second, I wavered. In the end, what was going to the MoD Wardingham archive going to achieve? Even if I did, somehow, find out who killed my parents, the knowledge would never bring them back. And I was putting everyone at risk in the attempt.

I could feel Ed and Ketty looking at me. Were they about to back out?

I turned my face away, suddenly knowing that I had to go, whatever the risks, even if I went by myself.

Ed's thoughts pushed into my mind.

I know you'll deny it if I say this out loud, but I can see on your face that you think we might not want to go with you to Wardingham.

I stared at him. He met my eyes.

We're all in this together, Dylan, he thought-spoke. *This is our next mission.*

He broke the connection.

'Thanks, Ed,' I said.

Harry stared at me, clearly bewildered.

'We need to make a plan,' Ketty said briskly. 'Once we're inside, what are we looking for?'

Everyone turned to me.

I cleared my throat, my thoughts coming into focus. 'My best guess is that my dad knew who was planning to kill him and told Bookman just before he died. Everyone thought my dad was being paranoid, but Bookman's murder kind of suggests there *is* a killer, who maybe knows that we're onto him and is desperately trying to get rid of everything that ties him to my parents' deaths.'

'. . . Ties that include the records of the conversation William Fox had with Bookman before he died?' Ed said. 'Records that will be stored somewhere at Wardingham?'

'Exactly,' I said.

We set off as soon as Laura reappeared from the bathroom. She agreed to drive us to the outskirts of Wardingham and let us approach the complex on foot.

Travelling through the middle of the night took very little time. We reached the drop-off point just after 3 a.m.

Laura rubbed her eyes and yawned. She must be exhausted from all the driving and worrying she'd done.

As we got out of the car, I went over and thanked her.

She pulled me into a hug. 'Please call me as soon as you're done, Dylan,' she said. 'I need to know you're all right.'

'Sure,' I said gruffly. I wasn't used to someone caring about me like that.

It felt weird.

Harry wished us luck, then raised his hand in a salute as we set off. I had hoped we'd get a chance to talk privately but, since leaving Bookman's house, he'd kind of been keeping his distance.

Whatever. There wasn't time to worry about it now.

Nico, Ed, Ketty and I watched Laura and Harry drive away, then set off across the first of the two fields we had to cross. It was a dark night – cold and overcast. No moon and hardly any stars were visible, but the Wardingham complex was easy to see. Lights were on across most of the first floor, as if a bright band had been wound round the building. It was an ugly concrete block on two floors altogether – squat and solid.

The two rings of fence were also visible – with more lights positioned over the entry hut by the gate. There was no sign of the armed guards. Presumably, they were inside the hut.

Full of misgiving, I turned to Ketty and whispered into the darkness. 'I don't suppose you've had a vision of us inside, have you?'

She shook her head. 'No, I've been trying, but it always gets harder when I'm stressed.'

'I've just counted four security cameras,' Ed hissed. 'And that's just the ones I can see from this angle.'

'We're going to have to take out the whole security operation,' Nico said. 'As we don't know how many guards there are, let's get one outside the hut on his own. Ed can mind-read him for data on the rest of the security system while the rest of us go into the hut and deal with whoever else is there. Okay?'

'Sure,' I said.

Ketty nodded.

As we drew closer, we stopped speaking. We didn't need to talk about how best to approach the hut. We'd worked together so many times it was obvious. Nico teleported a handful of stones into the air as we walked, then glanced round, making sure we were all ready.

Get your torch out. Ed's thought-speech appeared in my head, and vanished in an instant.

Torch? Oh, yeah, he meant my flashlight. As I pulled it out of my pocket, Nico teleported his stones so that they landed a few metres away from the hut.

The patter of the pebbles on the earth wasn't loud – but carried clearly across the night air. A guard appeared in the doorway, looking for the noise. He turned and drew the hut door shut. It was impossible to tell if anyone else was inside, but the website picture had shown two armed men.

We hid in the shadows, unseen. The guard crept towards the stones, peering round as he walked.

And then everything happened real quick. Nico teleported the guard up and flat on his back. The man fumbled for his gun. A moment later it was careering out of its holster and across the grass. The guard struggled to sit up. We ran towards him, Nico reached him first. Pushed him back as Ed arrived, making eye contact, doing his freaky hypno-mind-reading thing.

The whole thing took just seconds.

Nico rushed into the hut, Ketty and I at his heels. I had my force field fully primed, ready for the second guard, but the hut was empty.

I looked around. There was no sign that anyone else had been here – just a table and stool with a radio, a pile of old magazines and a cigarette lighter set along the only shelf.

Without speaking, Nico raced back outside to Ed.

'I guess the cutbacks we read about included letting go of the other security guard,' I said.

Ketty nodded.

I pointed to the security deck that sat on the table. It was a mass of knobs and buttons, with two CCTV screens above. Both showed pictures of the grass and wire fence beyond.

'Doesn't look like we're on camera,' I said.

Ketty glanced outside the hut, to where Ed was now attempting to hypnotise the guard into forgetting he'd seen us.

'Hope Ed's quicker on that man than he was with the guy at the last place,' Ketty said, fingering the deck.

'Guess we just have to wait it out.' I picked up the cigarette lighter from the shelf and flicked it on. 'Nico's got real good at telekinesis, hasn't he?' I murmured, trying to sound casual.

She nodded proudly. 'Yeah.' She smiled. 'But don't tell him. He's big-headed enough as it is.' She hesitated. 'I wish I could see something in the future, but I'm getting nothing.'

The old me would have undoubtedly made some crack about how 'seeing nothing' was nothing new for Ketty, but I didn't want to annoy her. I swallowed, then set the cigarette lighter back on the shelf. There was a question I needed to ask her.

'How do you feel about him?' I said quietly. 'Nico, I mean.'

Ketty's head shot up. She gave me a searching look.

'Why?' she said suspiciously.

'No reason,' I said. 'I just saw you guys after the scene in the garage with Milton and McKenna and I thought you looked . . . like a serious item.'

Ketty looked outside, to where Nico was staring at Ed in exasperation.

'I want to do the hypnosis first,' Ed was saying. 'It's more secure that way.'

'Sounds like a waste of time, man,' Nico insisted. 'Come on, you must be able to mind-read *something* to do with the security system.'

'A bit, but I can't see enough of his thoughts to be sure,' Ed said.

'Just tell me what you *can* see,' Nico said, sounding deeply irritated.

Ketty smiled.

'I really like Nico,' she said simply. 'And he says he really likes me.'

'Do . . . do you find yourself thinking about him a lot?' I said. 'Like . . . like caring what he thinks, and liking him even though sometimes he can be really annoying?'

Ketty smiled again. 'Are we still talking about me and Nico, or is this about you and Harry?'

Damn.

'No way,' I protested, alarmed she'd seen through me so easily. '*Course* not.'

'Okay, we're done.' Nico appeared in the hut doorway. 'There's definitely only one guard. Ed's finally got the guy in a deep sleep. Says he can only make it last half an hour, though.'

I made a face. That wasn't a lot of time.

'What about the security system?' Ketty asked.

'Ed says that button on the end turns off the power,' Nico said, pointing to the security deck. 'That's the fastest way to disable the electric fence and the cameras.'

I turned and found the button. A minute later we were through the gates to both rings of fences, and circling the building looking for a way in.

There were no windows at ground level and, so far, no door into the building.

'Here,' Ed said.

I shone my flashlight at where he was pointing . . . a huge front door.

'No sweat,' I said, standing back to let Nico open it with his telekinesis.

He studied the door for a second, then twisted his hand in front of it. Nothing happened.

'There's no electric current serving the lock, so I should be able to click it back,' he said.

I nodded, waiting. Nico's telekinesis had always worked before.

Nico flicked his wrist again. Still no movement in the door.

I glanced at the others. Ketty was staring at Nico, her

mouth open with alarm. Ed met my gaze, the same expression in his eyes.

And then, from the other side of the building, the sound of dogs barking erupted into the night air. I froze as, seconds later, two snarling Alsatians came racing around the corner towards us.

22: THE ARCHIVE

The noise was unbelievable. The two dogs were furious, barking their heads off. Nico was shouting nearly as loudly, his voice full of panic as he roared at them to get away.

I stared at him. Why wasn't he teleporting them over the fence? The same thought obviously struck Ketty.

'Telekinesis!' she screamed at him. 'Use your telekinesis!'

Immediately, Nico raised his hands. They shook as he focused on one of the dogs. It lifted off the ground, yelping in terror. As Nico moved it away from us, the other dog rushed forward. Nico quickly turned his attention to the second dog, but as he teleported that one away, the first dog was back on the ground, racing towards us again.

'Do something!' Ed yelled.

It took me a fraction of a second to realise he was shouting at me.

The door we'd been trying to access was right beside me. Why hadn't Nico's telekinesis unlocked it? I gave it an angry shove. To my amazement it opened.

Of course. How stupid we'd been! Shutting down the electricity had released everything automatically. Nico had been trying to unlock a door that was already unlocked!

'Guys!' I shouted. 'We're in.'

Nico turned to see the open door. In that moment he lost concentration. The nearest dog leaped forwards, past him, bounding up to Ketty. His paws reached her chest. With a shriek she fell backwards.

Now all hell broke loose. Everyone was yelling.

Nico was torn, turning between the dog that was snarling over Ketty and the one that he was keeping at bay.

'Focus on that one,' I yelled, pointing to the dog he was holding off. 'I'll deal with Ketty.'

Force field charged, I hurled myself at the Alsatian that was pinning Ketty to the ground. His mouth was clamped round her leg, his teeth piercing her sweats and skin.

For a second I gagged at the sight of the blood oozing through the material, then I gathered all my focus on my energy field and slid my hand into the dog's mouth. I made a fist and pushed, forcing my way to the back of the dog's throat. The dog made a choking sound, then released Ketty. He backed away from me snarling furiously. I was dimly aware of Nico beside me, teleporting the first dog over the fence and into the distant woods, but I kept my force field charged, and my focus on the dog right in front of me.

As soon as the first dog had disappeared, Nico dropped to his knees beside Ketty. Ed was already tearing open her sweats, examining the bite.

Out of the corner of my eye I could see Ketty, her face screwed up in pain. I kept my attention on the second dog, now padding backwards and forwards in front of me . . . wary of me . . . but coming closer again . . .

'We should get her to a hospital,' Ed said. 'She might need stitches and she should definitely have a tetanus jab.'

At the sound of his voice, my dog stopped pacing. He growled, then leaned back on his paws. *Jeez*, he was going to leap out at Ed.

'Nico,' I hissed. 'I need you to teleport this dog.'

But Nico wasn't listening. He was trying to help Ketty to her feet.

And then everything happened at once.

The dog pounced, jaws open and teeth bared. He flew past me, aiming straight at Ed . . . going for his throat.

I started to move, to hurl myself between Ed and the dog, but in that second I knew I wouldn't get there in time.

I also knew I had to protect Ed.

I reached out with my finger and channelled every ounce of my force field towards him. As I touched his shoulder, I could feel the energy flowing through me and out of me, circling his throat.

A split second later the dog reached Ed, but his teeth closed on air. He fell back with a whimper. My force field fell away from me altogether.

This time Nico was ready. In an instant he'd teleported the dog up and over the fence and into the woodland beyond.

The four of us stood, in shock, in silence.

Nico was bent over, panting. Ketty clung to his arm, her face unnaturally pale, the bloodstain on her left leg widening every second.

Ed was rigid with fear, his eyes wide and horrified.

'How did you do that, Dylan?' he said, his voice hoarse. 'That dog was going to kill me.'

I shrugged, as baffled as he was. 'I just focused on my force field . . . on making it go around you.' As I spoke, I reached out again, trying to repeat what I'd done before. I could feel the energy flowing through me – but it wasn't as strong as before . . . not vital enough to extend across another person. The more I pushed, trying to force it away from me, the weaker it grew.

'I can't do it again,' I said, suddenly feeling exhausted.

'We have to get Ketty to a doctor,' Nico said urgently. 'She's really hurt.'

Ed and I turned to them.

Ketty was leaning against Nico, wincing and clutching her leg. Blood was seeping through her sweatpants.

'Man, I'm so sorry, Ketts,' Nico was saying. 'Those dogs really freaked me out. I panicked until you yelled at me . . . forgot what I could do . . .'

Ketty shook her head. 'Don't—'

'Can you make it through the gate, babe?' Nico said. 'Wait, I'll teleport you and run underneath.'

'No,' I said. 'Let Ed go with her. He can call an ambulance from the road.'

'But I want to go with Ketty,' Nico said. 'I need to know she's going to be all right.'

'I'll be fine, Nico,' Ketty said crossly.

I stared at him. I had no idea what we were going to face inside the Wardingham building. At this point, Nico's psychic gift was going to be more useful than Ed's.

But how did I tell him that when his girl was bleeding in front of him? If it was Harry, I thought, I wouldn't want to send him off with someone else – even though, logically, Ed was as good a choice as anyone.

I'd want to be with him.

I pushed the thought out of my head.

Never mind freakin' Harry.

'*Please*, Nico. Dylan's right,' Ketty said. 'She needs your skills the most. I'll be fine with Ed.'

Nico hesitated, frowning.

'Come on, Nico,' I said fiercely. 'We've already been here far too long. We have to move.'

'I'll look after her.' Ed touched Nico's arm, then met his gaze.

Nico glazed over as the two boys communicated telepathically.

I don't know what Ed said in that private chat, but when he broke the connection, Nico had clearly made the decision to let Ketty go.

'Go on, then.' Nico gave Ketty a fierce hug, then teleported her over the fence and across the field beyond. I could just make out the edge of the road where Laura had dropped us. As Ketty sailed through the air towards that point, Ed ran through the gates after her.

'Keep checking in with us, yeah?' Nico yelled. 'Let me know how she is.'

'I will,' Ed yelled back. 'Don't forget you've only got about twenty-five minutes before that guard comes out of his hypnosis.'

That wasn't a lot of time.

Heart thumping, I gazed across the field beyond the building, watching Ketty travel through the air to the edge of road. Nico set her down. A second later, Ed ran up to her. He took out his phone, presumably to dial for a cab to take them to hospital.

'You don't think those dogs will come back, do you?' Nico said, looking worried.

'No. We'd have seen them if they'd come out of the woods.' I paused. 'I guess they brought in the dogs because of the staff cutbacks we read about . . . a replacement for the second guard.'

Nico nodded. 'We better get inside.'

Side by side, the two of us ventured through the open door. The building was cold and dark and echoey, a bleak length of corridor with a long stretch of bare wall on either side.

'We need to find stairs down to the basement,' I whispered.

Nico nodded. 'Over there.' He pointed to a set of concrete steps at the end of the corridor.

The basement was even colder and darker than the ground floor. Our flashlights revealed four large rooms, jammed with cupboards and storage shelving.

'How on earth do we know where to begin looking?' Nico said, staring round in bewilderment. 'The records on your dad's final meetings with Bookman could be anywhere.'

I marched across to the first shelf and picked up a piece of paper. It was a requisition – an order form – for a load of stationery.

My heart sank. 'There must be a key to the storage system somewhere . . . some way of working out where files are kept by date or name.'

'How about on that computer?' Nico pointed to a terminal in the corner.

'Great, except we've no electricity to power it.' I shivered.

Jeez. We had about twenty minutes until the guard outside came out of his hypnosis and what felt like a million miles of archive material to search.

And then footsteps ran towards us . . . a lean, male figure stood in the doorway, his flashlight weaving shadows across the wall opposite.

I froze. Before either Nico or I could act, the guy reached round and flicked a light switch. Three overhead fluorescent tubes hummed into instant action, flooding the room with light.

Harry stood in the doorway.

I stared at him, open-mouthed.

'I found a generator outside,' he said with a grin. 'See, Red? I told you I'd be useful.'

23: CLUSTERCHAOS

I stared at Harry, totally lost for words. Nico stood beside me, open-mouthed.

Harry's grin deepened. 'Hey, Red, we must stop meeting like this. Empty office buildings are not my idea of a party environment.'

'What the hell are you doing here?' I snapped.

'Mum refused to leave before. She wanted to be sure you got out okay, so we were still there when Ed and Ketty came out. Mum's taken them to the hospital. I thought, seeing as you were two guys down, I might be able to fill in.'

'For Pete's sake, Harry.' My irritation mounted. 'This isn't a freakin' game. You weren't supposed to hang around. You could get hurt.'

'Nice to know you care, Red.' Harry winked at me.

In spite of my annoyance, my heart gave a little lurch at that wink.

'I don't care,' I said, trying to sound as withering as possible. 'What I'm trying to say is that you can't be any use to us and if it comes to a fight, then Nico and I will have to protect you.'

'I can handle myself,' Harry said, an irritated edge now creeping into his voice. 'I got some power back into the building for you, didn't I? *And* I disabled the alarm. Plus, you know I've got other, shall we say specialist, IT skills.' He turned to Nico. 'I can get you inside the intranet here . . . through any terminal . . .'

'Really?' Nico sounded impressed. This just added to my annoyance.

'A bit of amateur hacking doesn't make you able to crack an MoD security system,' I said.

Harry pulled a CD from his pocket. 'This isn't amateur hacking,' he said. 'It's a proper program I downloaded off the net . . . brought it with me in case we needed it. It's called Clusterchaos . . . works like a cluster bomb, like lots of sub-bombs exploding all at once to break down a fire-wall in several places at a time *and*—'

'We don't want to destroy their security system, we just want to find the information about my dad.'

'Clusterchaos can do that. Once it's disarmed the fire-wall, you can find anything you want – across the whole intranet . . .'

'I don't—'

'Do it.' Nico spoke over me, to Harry, pointing to the terminal we'd spotted before.

'What are you *doing*?' I turned on Nico, furious.

'Harry sounds like he knows what he's talking about,'

Nico said. 'He managed to find and start the building's generator so we've got proper lights and power. We should give him a chance to do this.'

'But—'

'Get over yourself, *Red* . . .' Nico shot me a look – part irritation, part amusement. 'There's no way we can get through all the material in this archive doing a manual search, is there? Not in the twenty minutes we've got till the guard comes round. This is our best chance.'

The fact that this was true didn't make me any happier about letting Harry help us.

Seething, I followed Nico over to the computer. Harry had already switched on the hard drive and inserted his CD. Seconds later the screen started flashing with page after page of computer-program information.

'What's that?' I said.

'Clusterchaos is reading the security protocols,' Harry said. He leaned back in his chair. 'It'll take a few minutes.'

'It better not take any longer,' I muttered.

Nico was peering at the screen. 'Man, that is *cool*.' He turned to Harry, his eyes full of respect. 'How does it work?'

Harry explained, using terminology I didn't understand – and that I was sure Nico wouldn't be able to follow either. But Nico just nodded.

'Wow,' he said. 'Impressive.'

As Harry had predicted, after a couple of minutes the screen grew still. A single line of text flashed up: *Please enter your search terms*.

With a triumphant grin, Harry typed in my dad's name: *William Hamish Fox*.

A long list flashed up. Over one hundred entries.

'Too many,' I said. 'You need to narrow it down.'

'Okay, how about a date?' Harry said. 'Or a range of dates?'

I gave him the dates that covered the time from ten days before my dad's death to three days after.

This time the list was five items long.

Heart pounding, I scanned the information. The dates corresponded to the days in Mom's diary where she'd written *W to Hub*. Those were obviously the times when my dad had meetings with Bookman.

'Can you open those files?' I said.

'Sure.' Harry started tapping at the keyboard. 'It'll just take a couple of minutes.'

Nico was across the room, examining a folder of papers. I walked towards him, scanning the labels on the front of the filing cabinets as I passed.

Each cabinet had a number. I went around the room, taking in the cabinet labels 501–542.

The number Bookman had scratched in the ash at his feet leaped into my head.

343.

In all the rush to get here, I hadn't made the connection. If Bookman knew whoever killed him was on their way here, maybe the number was some sort of clue to what the killer was after.

I darted into the next room. The cabinets were all numbers in the low two hundreds. Higher numbers in the next room . . . up to 326.

I reached the next room. Filing cabinet 343 was the sixth cabinet along from the door. I yanked open the drawers. What was in here?

I pulled out a couple of files. A tally of MoD postal costs from 1982–1984 . . . some computer hardware instruction manuals . . . a bunch of spreadsheets . . .

I stood back, bewildered.

Harry appeared in the doorway. 'I've tried to open the five bits of data you want, but they're encrypted. They're small files, but it'll still take the best part of an hour to work out the decryption so I'm downloading them. We can look at them later.'

'Awesome,' I said. 'But I think I've found something else.'

I explained quickly about the number Bookman had written in the ash.

'I was certain it corresponded to this filing cabinet, but I can't find anything in here connected to my dad's meetings with Bookman.'

'Maybe the information is hidden,' Harry suggested. He reached past me and pulled a bundle of papers out of the cabinet. 'We should take everything. Examine it later.'

I went to help him, when another thought struck me. Surely it would have been real risky for Bookman to leave an important document in an open filing cabinet like this?

'Maybe the records Bookman hid here aren't *inside* the cabinet at all,' I said.

Harry stared at me. 'You mean . . .?'

'Let's pull it away from the wall.'

Heart in my mouth, I tugged at the cabinet. It was too heavy to move. Even with Harry's help I couldn't budge it.

'Nico!' I yelled.

He came running. 'Ed just contacted me remotely to say they're at the hospital. Ketty's okay,' he said breathlessly.

'Good,' I said. 'That's really great. Could you teleport this filing cabinet please?'

Nico shrugged. 'Okay, but we've only got twelve minutes until that guard comes out of the trance Ed put him into.'

Jeez, we were going to have to move fast.

With a flick of his wrist, Nico slid the cabinet away from the wall.

'What's this about?' he said.

I raced around to the back of the cabinet. Scanned it fast.

There, taped to the bottom corner, was a tiny disk.

My heart skipped a beat as I ripped the disk away from the metal. 'Look!' I held it up.

'We can play it on the computer in the other room while the encrypted files are downloading, see if it's relevant,' Harry said.

'It *must* be relevant,' I said.

The three of us raced back to the computer in the other room.

A red light was flashing over the door.

As Harry inserted the disk into the computer's drive, I turned uneasily to Nico.

'That light wasn't on before, was it? D'you think it's an alarm?'

'I don't know.' Nico shuddered. 'How much longer are the encrypted files going to take to download?'

'Two minutes max,' Harry said.

'We can easily see what's on this disk in two minutes,' I said. 'How long tile the guard wakes up?'

Nico checked his watch again. 'Seven minutes.'

My mouth was dry as the computer screen fizzled, then settled into a black and white CCTV picture of a hallway. It looked vaguely familiar.

'That's the Hub,' Harry said. 'I recognise it from the night I met you.'

I nodded. 'Yeah, it looks familiar to me, too.'

A man walked into view. He was wearing a shirt with the sleeves rolled up. He paced to the door, then turned.

I recognised him right away. A tall, middle-aged man with a long, straight nose and a slightly haughty expression.

'That's my dad,' I gasped.

'Ssh.' Nico put his hand on my arm. 'Listen.'

'*I can't let you do it,*' Dad was saying. '*I'm going to the police.*'

Another person spoke, but too quietly to make out what they said, or even if the low mumble belonged to a man or a woman.

'Turn up the volume,' I said desperately.

'It *is* up,' Harry hissed. '*Shh.*'

'*Then you'll have to kill me,*' Dad said. He spread his arms wide and smiled. '*Kill me and leave a wife distraught and a daughter without a father.*' He paused. '*You're not going to do that. I know you're not.*'

He stood, still standing and smiling. Still utterly confident that he was not going to be hurt. And, without a shadow of a doubt, I knew that I was about to see him die.

24: SHOWDOWN

Harry was saying something in a low voice to Nico, but I couldn't tear my eyes away from the screen.

My dad was looking at someone. His killer.

The killer was talking, but still in a low, indecipherable mumble.

'Dylan?' Harry tugged at my arm. 'The Clusterchaos program has finished downloading the encrypted files. Let's take the disk and look at it somewhere else.'

'Wait.' I wrenched my arm away. On screen my dad was backing away from his attacker.

'*But I know what you're planning,*' he said. '*I can't let you get away with it.*'

And then the killer stepped into view. A trim, suited woman with a neat blonde bob. Even before she turned I knew who she was.

Geri.

Beside me Nico tensed. I stared, glued to the screen.

'*I'm sorry, William.*' Geri's voice was angry and clipped.

She raised the gun in her hand and pointed it at my dad. '*You don't have the right to stop this . . . to stop me.*'

The shot rang out. A single bullet. Into my dad's chest. He crumpled to the floor, his eyes shut.

Geri stood, watching for a second, then she turned and walked past the camera, out of sight.

I stared at my dad's lifeless body as the screen fizzled to nothing.

The silence in the room thundered in my ears.

'Guys, we *really* need to get out of here now. We've got less than two minutes to get past the guard,' Harry hissed. He pressed the disk drive and handed me the minidisk.

Nico turned to me with shocked eyes.

'I can't believe . . . *Geri* . . .' he tailed off.

I nodded, shoving the minidisk into my pocket. I was unable to believe it myself.

'Dylan. Nico. We—' As Harry spoke, the lights went out and the computer lost power.

I glanced through the door. The electricity was totally down through the whole floor.

'Someone's turned off the generator,' Harry whispered.

'That guard must be inside,' Nico whispered. He grabbed my arm. '*Dylan.* We have to hide.'

I let myself be dragged across the room. The three of us crouched behind a row of filing cabinets.

My head was spinning. *Geri* killed my dad.

All this time *she* was the murderer. She had come to me

and recruited me and befriended me and made me feel I was a bit more special than the others – and all the time she had killed my dad.

I suddenly remembered what Laura had said about Mom's fears for her own safety, after Dad died.

Oh. My. God.

Geri had killed my mom as well.

It was too much to take in. Too horrific to let myself believe.

And yet I'd seen the evidence.

Footsteps echoed along the corridor towards us.

And then the door slowly opened.

I froze as Geri Paterson herself walked into the room.

Shock gave way to a fury that filled me from the toes up.

No way was I hiding from her . . . evil cow.

I stood up. Harry grabbed at my arm, trying to pull me back, but I stepped out from behind the filing cabinet, out of his reach.

'You murdering bitch,' I said.

'Ah, Dylan, dear, I thought you must be here.' Geri spoke from the doorway, her flashlight shining in my eyes. 'Where's Nico?'

With a roar, Nico reared up, arms outstretched. The filing cabinet opposite him soared into the air.

Geri fired. Not an actual gun. Some sort of tranquilliser. The dart hit Nico in the chest. He fell to the floor, unconscious. The filing cabinet he'd been teleporting landed on the ground with a thud.

'What did you do to him?' I said, all my fury evaporating in shock.

'He'll be out for twenty minutes or so,' Geri said dismissively. 'And I know Ed and Ketty are in the hospital. They phoned me. So it's just you and me, Dylan.' She looked round the room. 'From your earlier greeting may I take it that you found the minidisk Bookman hid here?'

'You killed my dad,' I said, tears rising in my eyes. '*And* my mom.'

Geri lowered the flashlight so I could see her face. Her expression was cold and cruel.

'I have been a senior-level government agent for over twenty years,' she said. 'I brought together the scientist behind the Medusa gene and the resources to develop it. Along the way I've done many things you wouldn't understand. Now where's the minidisk, Dylan?'

'I don't know,' I lied, feeling the disk in my pocket as I spoke.

I braced myself for Geri to threaten me, but instead she stepped briskly forward, took one of Nico's legs and dragged him to the door.

All of a sudden Ed surged into my head.

Dylan, what's going on? I can't reach Nico? Are you out of the building? The guard will be coming round any second.

It's Geri. I let everything she'd done flood rapidly through my mind as Geri dumped Nico's unconscious body by the door and went through his pockets.

Ed listened with a growing sense of horror.

222

But that means she must have killed Bookman, too. I'm calling the police.

There's no point. You know Geri will be able to talk her way out of anything with the police.

It's the only hope.

He broke the connection.

For a second I wondered if Ed was right . . . hope surged inside me. Then it died.

Calling the police wasn't enough. Geri had proved time and again that the police were, ultimately, under her control and at her disposal. I was going to have to find a way to escape – and get justice – by myself.

I focused on my force field. Harry must still be somewhere in the room, but he was unarmed and without a psychic skill.

My ability to protect myself was the only chance we had.

I was expecting Geri to raise her tranquilliser gun and aim it at me, but instead she yanked open the nearest filing cabinet drawer and scattered the papers on the floor. She turned to me, her flashlight burning my eyes.

'I want that minidisk. Now,' she spat.

'No,' I said, my earlier fury returning with full force.

Geri sighed. She tucked the tranquilliser gun back in its holster and drew a real gun from her jacket. She pointed the gun at Nico's head.

'I know that you can withstand a bullet, Dylan, dear, but I don't think Nico will stand much of a chance, will he?'

'You won't shoot him!' I said. 'It's *Nico*.'

'I shot Bookman earlier,' Geri snapped. 'An unconscious boy would be no problem after that.'

I suddenly remembered how we'd spoken to Geri just after finding Bookman's dead body. How I'd heard plates clattering in the background.

'I thought you were in the Lake District, with Alex and Jez,' I said.

'I was just down the road.' Geri chuckled – her high, tinkly laugh. 'It's amazing how suggestive the power of sound is . . . now give me the disk or Nico dies. Right here. Right now.'

She cocked her gun and held it against Nico's temple.

I still couldn't believe she would really kill him. But after everything else I'd found out today, I also knew I couldn't take the chance.

Whichever way I looked at it, Geri had me totally in her power.

Gritting my teeth, I fished the minidisk out of my pocket and held it towards her. Rage flooded my whole body.

'Why did you kill my parents?' I said, my voice shaking with fury. If I had to give up the proof, at least I was going to get some answers.

'It was their own fault,' Geri said. 'Your dad provoked me.'

'How d'you freakin' figure that?' I said. 'I've just seen evidence that shows my dad was totally defenceless.'

'What, the old CCTV footage from the Hub on this?' Geri said smoothly, stepping forward to take the minidisk. 'This shows that your dad was blackmailing me.'

'*What*?' I said.

Geri stepped smartly back and aimed her gun at Nico's head again. 'Your father discovered something the Medusa Project was planning to do.'

'What was that?'

'It doesn't matter now,' Geri said. 'All you need to know is that your father didn't like our plan and was threatening to expose the whole project. I know you won't understand this, Dylan, but he left me no choice but to kill him.'

'You *evil cow*,' I said, hot tears filling my eyes. 'And what about my mom? I suppose you're going to say she was getting in your way, too?'

'No. Your airhead mother didn't know about the project your dad wanted to expose,' Geri said with a sneer. 'She suspected me of killing him, though. She stole this disk containing the CCTV of our argument. Bookman and I had to get it back. You're mother wouldn't give it up without a fight.'

'A fight which you made look like suicide.' I felt sick.

'Yes. If Bookman hadn't kept the film and put it on this disk, your mother wouldn't have needed to die. It was his fault . . . stupid man threatening to blackmail me. He managed to keep the disk away from me afterwards, too. He said it was his insurance policy . . . a way of making sure I guaranteed him a comfortable old age. That's why I killed him earlier. He'd kept this disk hidden away here for years. All the while he told me there was some elaborate set-up whereby if I did away with him, Milton and

225

McKenna would come after me.' Geri paused. 'It was you, Dylan, who led me to the truth . . . ironic really, considering I was trying to stop you with those texts . . .'

'That was *you*?'

'Yes, but the texts didn't work and on you went and, eventually, you led me to Milton and McKenna. Of course, once we actually had the two of them in custody, I realised that they had no idea about your father's death . . . no idea about me . . . Bookman had been bluffing all along. I wasn't sure what to do at first, but once you started asking about Bookman, I knew it was only a matter of time before the truth came out. Which meant I had to find this disk before you did – whatever it took.'

I stared at her, rage coursing through every cell of my body. I couldn't believe what an idiot she'd made of me . . . Every time I'd turned to her for help I'd played right into her hands.

'So you killed Bookman so he couldn't blackmail you any more, just like you killed my dad and my mom to stop them talking . . .' I paused. 'Except my mom didn't actually know anything real important about your work . . . nothing she could prove anyway . . . Once you had the disk back from her, you could have just threatened her not to talk.'

'I didn't want to leave any loose ends,' Geri said briskly. 'And, of course, dear, your parents are not really in the same category. Your father was a genius whose passing was a terrible loss to the world of science, whereas your mother was a pretty, silly little East Coast princess with a diary full of beauty appointments. Plus, of course, she was going to die anyway . . . because of the Medusa gene.'

'Shut up about my mom!' I shouted. 'You don't know what you're talking about.'

I lowered my face and glanced quickly sideways, hoping against hope that I would catch a glimpse of Harry.

Nothing but darkness.

I looked back at Geri. She was still aiming her gun in Nico's direction, but her eyes were on me. If I could just move fast enough, maybe I could reach her before she shot him. Maybe I could even wrestle the gun off her.

'You know I can protect myself against a bullet,' I said, taking a step closer to Geri. 'And you can't keep me and Nico down here forever. It must be nearly morning . . . people will be coming to work in a few hours. Plus, there's a guard outside . . .'

'I shot the guard with a tranquilliser dart, just like I did Nico,' Geri said. 'They'll both be out for another fifteen minutes. Which is more time than I need.'

'More time than you need to do what?' I said, edging closer again.

Geri put the disk in her bag.

'More time than I need to make sure that you and Nico are dead,' she said.

25: THE MURDER PLAN

I gasped. Was Geri serious?

'You won't kill me and Nico,' I said. 'You *need* us. We're your Medusa Project.'

'You've become more trouble than you're worth,' Geri said bitterly. 'After this, I want nothing more to do with any of you. You and Nico won't really be missed. Well, Fergus may make a fuss for a while, but I can handle him.'

'What about my aunt and uncle?' I said desperately.

Geri smiled pityingly at me. 'We both know they couldn't give a fig about you, dear.' She sighed. 'I suppose you've already been in remote contact with Ed?'

'No,' I lied.

'I don't believe you.' Geri sighed again. 'Which means, of course, that Ed and Ketty will have to be dealt with, too . . .'

Was she threatening to kill them as well?

Geri held up the minidisk and smiled . . . 'Still, so long

as I've got this, there's no proof I ever did anything against the law.'

'Then killing us doesn't make sense,' I protested. 'We'll be found and . . . and . . . people will know you were here. There are cameras . . . alarm lights were going off earlier . . .'

'You disabled the cameras when you came in, remember? And the red flashing light above the door was just an emergency light panel,' Geri said. 'I must have arrived outside the building shortly after you'd turned on the generator. I have to say I was impressed, Dylan. I knew Ed would hypnotise the guard, but I was banking on you not knowing about either the guard dogs or the generator.' She smiled. 'I had no idea you were capable of such a clever move: shutting down the main power supply to get inside the building, then activating the back-up so you could operate properly inside.'

Again, I wondered where Harry was. It was him who'd found the generator and managed to get it working.

I shook myself. It didn't matter. I had to try and catch Geri unawares myself . . . make a leap for the gun . . .

'There's just one more thing,' Geri said. 'I want the code for the Medusa gene.'

I stared her in the eye. 'I destroyed it,' I lied.

'I don't believe you.' Geri drew a hand-held scanner – a smaller version of the one Jack had used – from her pocket. She held the scanner towards me. Instinctively, I surrounded my whole body with my force field.

Geri laughed her high, tinkly laugh. 'This is a very powerful reader,' she said. 'It can pick up the microchip's signal from four metres away. Your force field can't touch it – just wait for the beep.'

The microchip reader remained silent. Geri's smile faded. She pointed the reader at Nico, then looked up at me, her mouth set in a thin line.

'Destroying that code was foolish, Dylan.'

'No way,' I snarled. 'Foolish would have been letting a toxic cow like you have it.'

Geri waved her hand dismissively, then stepped backwards, into the doorway. She was still pointing the gun at Nico. 'Goodbye.'

My heart thudded. I was still at least two metres away from her. No way could I reach her before she pulled the trigger. I took another small step forwards. I *had* to buy more time. 'What are you going to do?' I said.

Geri indicated all the filing cabinets she'd emptied . . . the contents strewn across the floor.

'A couple of kids came into the building last night. They knocked out the guard, smashed up the security systems and got into the basement. Then they vandalised a bunch of files . . .'

She stood, the door handle in her gloved hand.

'Then what?' I said, edging forward again. 'You're just going to leave us here?'

'As you pointed out earlier, I can't kill you with a bullet, Dylan, and a bomb would attract too much attention,' Geri said. 'This way you'll be trapped and the Wardingham defence system itself will kill you.'

'What d'you mean?'

Geri laughed her false, high laugh again. 'The floor plans from the file at Bookman's house were most helpful,' she said mysteriously. 'On top of which, I don't even have to lock the door. There's a fire hydrant out here that you "vandals" were messing about with. It fell and jammed the door from the outside, preventing you from getting out of the room . . .'

I frowned. Geri had already said that the guard would be coming round in fifteen minutes. So what if we were trapped in the archive room for a while? What on earth was she planning?

Geri shot me a final, enigmatic smile, then left, pulling the door shut behind her.

I raced towards it. As I grabbed the handle, there was a thud outside. Was that Geri, jamming the door? Yes, it was totally stuck. I rattled the handle again, tugging for all I was worth.

The door stayed firmly shut.

I seized my flashlight and crouched beside Nico. He was out cold. I shook him, but there was no response. Geri had said he'd be unconscious for another fifteen minutes. At least then he'd be able to shift whatever was blocking our way out.

I put my ear against the door. There was no sound from outside. Geri had left. I turned back to the room.

'Harry?' I whispered.

'Has she really gone?' His voice was shaken.

I'd never been happier to hear anything in my life.

'I think so. Are you okay?' I said.

'I'm fine.' I could hear him moving across the room. 'I hid over in the corner by the air vent.'

I turned my flashlight, finding him in the darkness. He was picking his way across the filing cabinet Geri had tipped onto the floor. He reached the door and pushed at the handle.

'It's stuck,' he said.

'I know. Maybe if we both try, we could ram it open.'

We stood together. Harry counted to three. I engaged my force field and we slammed our shoulders against the door. It barely moved.

Harry stood back, panting. 'Nico told me you drilled your way through a wall when you were on a mission in Africa,' he said. 'Won't your force field work here?'

'My force field just protects me,' I explained. 'It doesn't mean I'm able to get through every type of material and this door's made of something stronger than plasterboard. Plus, it took all the others to get me through that wall back in Africa.'

I shone my flashlight around the room, hoping against hope that I might see a window we hadn't noticed before. But there was nothing.

'I don't get it,' I said. 'Why leave us all down here? I mean the power's out, but all we have to do is sit tight and at worst, we'll get let out in a few hours, free to tell our side of the story.'

'She said she was going to kill you.' Harry shuddered. 'I don't think she was bluffing.'

'Okay, but how?'

'I don't know.'

My mind ran, rapidly, over ways in which Geri might think she could hurt me. She knew everything about my ability except the way, earlier tonight, I'd managed to extend my force field beyond myself to protect another person.

'She knows I can survive things I can see coming,' I said.

Harry stared at me. 'What about things you *can't* see?'

'What d'you mean?'

'Come with me.' Harry grabbed my hand and raced to the far corner of the room. My flashlight created jerky shadows as I ran past rows of filing cabinets. Harry pointed to a tiny space between the final cabinet and the end of the room. A grille was fixed to the bottom of the wall. He pointed to its bars. 'There.'

'This is where you hid?' I said, wondering if he'd gone mad. 'Why are you showing me?'

Harry turned to me, exasperated. 'Don't you get it, Red? It's a danger you can't see.'

I stared at him, running through the options in my mind. What danger would I not be able to see? Not solid objects. Not fire. Not water . . .

'Oh my God,' I said. I looked down at the air vent, then

held my hand over the thin metal bars that covered it. A slight draught cooled my palm. I turned to Harry, the horror of the situation hitting me fully.

'It's gas,' I said. 'She's sending in poison gas to kill us.'

26: BREATHING

As we watched the vent, I caught the faintest scent of disinfectant.

Was that the poison gas? I backed away from the wall.

'This gas must be what Geri was referring to when she said the Wardingham defence system would kill us,' Harry said.

'You mean these vents were designed to release gas into the room?' I said.

Harry gave a grim nod. 'It's a way of dealing with intruders, I guess.' He bit his lip. 'At least we've worked out what it is before it kills us.'

'Awesome.' I turned to him, panic rising. 'We're going to die. All we need to figure out now is when.'

Harry stared at the air vent. He sniffed, breathing in. 'Can you smell that . . . that . . . like a swimming pool smell?'

I nodded. 'What are we going to do?'

'Your force field can protect you, can't it?' Harry said

anxiously. 'That gives us a chance to get out of here. I mean, maybe it'll make me unconscious for a while before it's actually fatal, and in the mean time—'

'You don't understand,' I said. 'The energy force I put around myself doesn't provide air for me to breathe. I still need oxygen. My force field offers zero protection against poison gas.'

Harry backed away from the vent, his eyes darting around the room. 'But this isn't a big space,' he said, 'We've probably only got a few minutes. Geri Paterson said it would take less than a quarter of an hour, remember?'

His eyes rested on me again . . . I couldn't bear to see the horror that filled them.

'We're going to find a way out of here,' I said.

'How?' Harry's voice rose. 'There are no windows and the door is jammed. The only other way out is through the air vent – and that's precisely where the gas is coming from.' He coughed. 'God, the smell's getting stronger.'

It was – an acrid stench, like bleach.

I backed further away from the air vent, trying to clear my head so I could think it through logically. My thoughts returned to the African prison we'd been holed up in a few weeks ago – and how the others had used me as a battering ram to force a way through the thin, hollow wall. Maybe the walls here would be really flimsy, too. After failing to punch through the door, I didn't hold out much hope, but it was worth a try.

Using all my strength, I struck the wall in front of

me. Solid. Even with Harry's help I wouldn't make a dent in it.

Holding his breath, Harry pulled off his jacket, ran forward and shoved it over the air vent. He raced back to my side, pulling out his phone. 'That's not going to stop the gas, just slow it down. I'm going to call my mum. I want her to know what . . . what's going to happen . . .'

'Wait a second.' I glanced desperately around the room again. An idea was clawing at the edges of my mind. 'The room is a box,' I said.

'*What*?' Harry held out his hands in disbelief. 'What are you *talking* about?'

'The room is a box . . .' I muttered again. 'A box has six sides . . . four walls . . . a floor.' I looked up. 'The ceiling.'

Harry followed my gaze. 'The *ceiling*?'

'Yes.' The ceiling was made up of styrofoam panels. There would probably be a gap between the panels and the floor of the room above. If Harry and I could move one panel, then maybe we could somehow climb inside the ceiling, drag Nico up with us and replace the panel. If it would keep out the gas, then we'd at least buy ourselves a little more time.

I explained my idea to Harry.

For a moment he looked at me as if I was crazy. 'But how the hell are we going to get up into the ceiling and replace the panel, even if we can remove it?'

'I don't know, but have you got a better idea?'

We looked at each other for a second, then Harry shook his head.

'No,' he said. 'I don't. Come on. Help me get up on top of this filing cabinet.'

I helped him climb up, then rushed over to Nico while Harry pressed gently around the edges of the panel immediately above his head. Nico was still out cold. As I straightened up from his body, I caught another, stronger scent of bleach. As I breathed it in, my head spun. The poison gas was starting to work.

'We don't have much time,' I said.

'I know,' Harry grunted. 'I can smell it, too.' He pushed at the panel above his head. With a faint screech, it shifted.

'Look!' Harry exclaimed.

I looked. There was a sixty-centimetre gap above the ceiling, criss-crossed by metal girders that looked easily strong enough to bear our weight.

'See?' I said. 'It's going to work.' I dragged Nico across the floor to the filing cabinet while Harry carefully lifted the panel out of position.

'Help me get Nico up there.'

Harry jumped down. Together we lifted Nico into a standing position. I propped him against the cabinet, while Harry climbed back up on top. He reached down to heave Nico up. But even with me pushing with all my strength from beneath, it was impossible to move him. He was a dead weight.

By the time we'd had two or three tries at getting Nico on top of the cabinet, the bleach smell filled the air. I was starting to feel light-headed.

'You look like you might faint, Red.' Harry said anxiously. 'D'you feel okay?'

'Awesome.'

'Liar.' He paused, making a face. 'I feel really weird, too. I don't think this is going to work. Even if we could move Nico, it's taking too long for us to climb. By the time we're all up above the ceiling, the gas will be up there, too.'

I stared at him. He was right. I could feel the gas working on me, making it hard to think. How much longer did we have until it left Harry and me as unconscious as Nico?

'Wait. Get down here, I've got an idea.'

Without a word, Harry slid back down to the ground. 'You know . . . I was thinking . . . this gas probably isn't traceable.' He coughed, then blinked, clearly trying hard to focus. 'The police are going to turn up and we're just going to be dead and there won't be any clues about what happened and that woman . . . Geri Paterson . . . she's going to have got away with *all* of it. Your dad and your mum and . . . and us, too.'

'No.' I hauled myself past him, up onto the cabinet. 'Geri's not getting away with any of it. We're going to get out of here and I'm going to track her down and make her pay.' I reached up, through the gap in the panels that Harry had made. The girder immediately above me was wide enough to hook my knee over. I pulled myself up, then crouched on the metal bar, shining my flashlight along the space above. The boards that formed the floor to another room were just a few centimetres over my head. Summoning

239

all my energy, I created a force field around my fist and punched upwards. My hand smacked against the wood. It didn't even leave a scratch.

Still crouching, I moved to the next girder. More floor-boards above my head. I shone the flashlight along a bit further. The smell of bleach was real strong now. I held my breath and moved along again.

I shone my flashlight into the corner of the space. A large, square, aluminium pipe met my eyes. An air vent leading to the room above. I knew the vent into our room was contaminated, but surely the poison gas wouldn't have reached the floor above yet. I wriggled across the girders, still holding my breath. I reached the metal air vent, made a fist and punched at the nearest seam. It shook.

That was a start. I punched again. And again. The vent was only made of thin aluminium. Another punch and it cracked at the top . . . another punch . . . another crack . . .

I took a quick breath. It made my head spin. I summoned the force field again, and slammed my fist, hard, right into the heart of the biggest crack. With a snap the piping came apart. I gripped the sharp aluminium sides, forcing them far enough back so that I had room to crawl through.

'Harry!' I yelled. 'I've found a way out.'

'You go on.' His voice sounded really weak. 'I . . . I can't . . .'

I hesitated for a second. Should I go back?

No. Harry's best chance was for me to get out of here and make my way back downstairs as fast as I could.

Force field fully charged, I hauled myself into the vent. The walls were tight against my body. I crawled, commando style, as fast as I could. The pipe sloped upwards. Totally dark.

And then I felt a blast of cooler air coming from up ahead. It was lighter there, too. I must be coming to another room. I risked a breath.

The air was much cleaner.

Straight ahead of me was an aluminium grille, like the one the gas was coming through in our room below.

Force field engaged, I punched at the bars with all my might. One. Two.

I broke through on the third punch. Grabbing the outside of the grille, I hurled myself through, slithering onto the floor of the room on the other side.

I got to my feet and raced to the door. I ran left. Dead end. I turned right. Stairs.

I pounded down to the basement level again, hoping the room Harry and Nico were still trapped in would be easy to spot.

It was. As I leaped off the bottom step, I saw the fire extinguisher Geri had jammed against our door handle.

I raced over and hurled it out of the way. I flung open the door. The powerful smell of the poison gas hit me straight away. Harry was on the floor beside Nico, his head hanging between his knees. He looked up as I ran over to them.

'Hey, Red.' He forced a smile, then slumped into un-consciousness at my feet.

27: PROTECTION

'Harry!' I yelled his name in his ear. 'Wake up!'

But Harry was out cold.

Holding my breath, I turned from him to Nico. Which one should I move first?

I hesitated for a split second, then grabbed Nico round the legs and dragged him outside. He'd been unconscious for what seemed like ages, now. At least Harry had only just passed out. Hopefully, he'd be okay for a few moments.

I was desperate for air by the time I reached the corridor. I gasped in a breath. The bleach-smelling gas was out here now, acrid in the back of my throat, but not anywhere near as strong as it was inside the room. I deposited Nico halfway down the corridor where the air seemed clearer, then raced back for Harry.

As I entered the room again, my top clinging sweatily to my back, Ed pushed his way into my head.

Dylan, what's happening?

Not now.

Ketty's fine and the police should be there . . .

They're not. Geri must have got to them. Please, Ed, let me go.

We're on our way.

Ed broke the connection as I reached Harry.

I gripped him under the arms and heaved him outside. He was about the same height as Nico, but stockier and heavier. My arms felt like they were being pulled out of their sockets by the time I reached the door. I stopped for a second to shut it behind me, then lugged him down the corridor.

I reached Nico, deposited Harry beside him then slumped to the ground myself. I sat on the cold floor in the silent corridor, my head in my hands.

'Dylan?' Nico croaked. I turned my flashlight on his face. He screwed up his eyes against the glare. 'What happened?' he gasped.

I shook my head, too exhausted to speak.

Nico turned his head and saw Harry lying beside him, eyes tight shut. He struggled onto his side.

'Where are we?' he said, still sounding hoarse. 'What's the matter with Harry?'

I leaned over, touching Harry's face. His eyes were still shut. I bent lower, so my cheek was just above his mouth and nose.

My heart skipped a beat. 'I don't think he's breathing.'

'What?' Nico sat up, wincing, his forehead clutched in his hand. 'What happened?'

Adrenaline surged through me. 'Geri gassed us. I thought you had it worse, but maybe Harry was taking deeper breaths.'

Nico stared at me, bewildered. I bent closer over Harry. I couldn't work out if he was breathing or not. My head was still spinning – I wasn't sure whether it was from the gas or all my efforts to save the three of us.

Still, one thing was certain. Harry was deathly pale.

Laura's anxious face swam in front of my mind's eye. Then Harry's own smile.

My heart twisted into a knot.

I *had* to save him. Nothing mattered more.

My mind raced back to the resuscitation class Alex had given us. Desperately trying to remember what she'd told us, I took Harry's nose between the finger and thumb of one hand. I stared at his face. There was something you were supposed to do with the chin, too, wasn't there? Why hadn't I paid more attention?

Keep the airway clear, that was it, wasn't it? Grabbing Harry's chin, I tilted his head slightly back. Then I leaned over him, took a deep breath and breathed the air into his mouth. Again. Again.

Harry spluttered. I jerked back, giving him space.

He coughed again, his eyes opening.

He blinked at me, his eyes crinkling into a smile. 'We made it,' he croaked.

I smiled back.

Harry shifted onto his elbows, closer to my face. 'Hey, were you kissing me just then, Red?'

I could feel my smile deepening. I felt like crying with relief.

'In your dreams,' I said.

'Excuse me,' Nico said pointedly. 'But the gas smell out here's getting worse. I think we should move.'

I nodded, my face reddening slightly.

The three of us scrambled to our feet. The two boys still looked pale and a little unsteady. We made our way along the corridor and up the stairs to the ground floor. As we walked, I filled the others in on exactly what had happened. Harry was clearly impressed by everything I'd done. Nico was thoughtful . . . silent.

Outside the sky had lightened slightly. Almost dawn. The air was cold and clear. I took several deep breaths, not minding the goosebumps that covered my arms as the breeze blew around us.

The guard was lying outside where we'd left him. His eyes were closed, but he was stirring. As we stood over him, Nico turned to me.

'This isn't good,' he said in a low voice. 'Geri has done everything she can to cover her tracks. She wants us dead and, as things stand, she'll know we're alive.'

'What are you saying?' I said. 'D'you think she's going to come after us? Try to kill us again?'

'I think it's highly likely,' Nico said. 'Geri doesn't like loose ends.'

The guard at our feet gave a low moan.

'So what are you going to do?' Harry asked.

Nico looked at me. He raised his eyebrows.

I nodded, slowly, realising what he was suggesting. 'We need to cover our tracks,' I said. 'Make it look like we died here.'

'That's crazy,' Harry said.

'I don't mean make out *you* died, just me and Nico.' I said. 'Geri doesn't even know we're in touch with you.'

'I know. I mean, it's crazy for you all to cut yourself off from the rest of the world like that,' Harry said.

'The rest of the world thinks we're dead anyway,' Nico said.

'What?' Harry said.

'It's true,' I said. 'We're not on any databases. It's only Geri and our families who know we're alive.'

'The only question is how,' Nico said.

I glanced at the guard again, an idea popping into my head.

'Just give me a sec,' I said.

I rushed into the guard's hut. Was it really only a short while ago that Ketty and I had stood in here, talking about how she felt about Nico? How I felt about Harry?

I scanned the shelf, looking past the magazines for the cigarette lighter I remembered seeing here before.

There.

I grabbed the lighter and raced outside. I thrust it at Nico.

'Take off your jacket,' I said. 'We need to set light to it, then you need to teleport it into the building,' I said.

'Why?' Nico frowned. 'What's that going to do?'

'That's insane, Red,' Harry said – a note of admiration in his voice.

'I don't understand,' Nico said.

'When the fire meets the gas, there'll be an explosion,' I explained. 'In the mess that's created no one will know if we were inside the building or not.'

Nico's eyes widened. For the first time since he'd come round he looked properly awake.

'Brilliant.' He took the lighter and flicked it on.

'What about him?' Harry pointed to the guard who was moaning more loudly now, his eyelids fluttering.

I put my hand on Nico's arm. 'Teleport him away from here first.'

Nico raised his hand. With a twist, the guard was lifted into the air. Nico zoomed him up and through the night air. He deposited him about two hundred metres from the building, near the place where he had left Ketty earlier.

The sight of that spot clearly reminded Nico of Ketty, too. He turned to me anxiously. 'Have you heard from Ed?' he said. 'Is Ketty, okay?'

'Yes,' I said. 'They're fine and they're on their way here now.'

'Good.' Nico turned back to the lighter and held it under his jacket.

'We should stand further back,' Harry said.

We ran back about fifty metres, to the edge of the trees. Nico tied his jacket into a knot and set it ablaze. He held up both hands and sent the jacket zooming back towards the building. It flew over the two fences and in through the front door which we'd left open.

I waited, every muscle tensed, waiting for the blast.

Nothing happened. Long seconds passed.

Nico took a step forward. 'It's not going off,' he said. 'Maybe I didn't send it far enough.'

'Maybe the fire burned itself out,' Harry suggested.

'Damn.' Nico took another step forward. Then another.

Harry and I followed. We were only thirty metres or so from the house, now.

'Be careful,' I said. 'It could go off any—'

A series of loud booms sounded from the building. I froze as a ball of fire ballooned out the front door.

Beside me, Nico's mouth dropped open. 'That's massive,' he gasped. 'That's *really*—'

Another huge blast rocked the whole building. Black smoke appeared at the first-floor windows.

'It's going to—!'

BOOM!

The building exploded. A massive fireball erupted out of the roof and windows. It hurtled towards us like a rocket. All fire and smoke and heat.

Right at us in less than a second. There was no time to run. It was coming too fast.

'No!' I reached out and grabbed the others by the wrists. With every cell in my body I directed my force field across my own skin and from there to Nico and Harry.

Protect us all, I willed the energy that flowed from inside me.

Protect us. Please.

28: THE FUTURE

I steeled myself for the impact of the fire, totally focused on the energy I was creating around me and Nico and Harry.

A second later the flames surrounded us. I kept every nerve focused on my force field, pushing away the fire.

The flames licked at our faces . . . smoke billowed . . . pieces of wood and brick flew in front of our eyes . . .

And then everything was gone, the fire sucking past us and into the air and the bits of the building slamming down on the ground all around us.

I released the force field and stood, feeling the energy still ricocheting around my body.

'Is everyone okay?' Nico asked.

Harry nodded. He looked at me, totally stunned. 'How did you do that?'

'I don't know,' I said. 'I just let go of everything . . . it was almost like I was doing it on instinct. Not trying . . .'

'That was unbelievable, Dylan,' Nico said shakily. 'And way beyond cool.'

I looked around. The scene around us was one of complete devastation. The top of the building was blown clean off and the rest a burning shell.

'The police will be here soon,' Nico said.

'Ed and Ketty should be here sooner,' I said.

'Let's wait in those trees,' Nico went on.

I'd only gone a couple of steps before I realised Harry wasn't with us. He was still standing, staring, open-mouthed, at the bombsite in front of him. I went back and touched his arm gently.

'Harry?' I said. 'We need to get under cover of the trees.'

He turned and stared at me, his eyes wide with wonder. 'You just saved all our lives,' he said.

'Yeah, I'm awesome like that,' I smiled. 'Come on.'

Harry followed me. As we reached the trees, Laura drove up with Ketty and Ed in the back of the car. As we got in, Laura gaped at the devastation behind us.

'What on earth . . .?'

'We have to go,' I urged.

The sound of sirens filled the air. Laura cast an anxious glance at her son, gritted her teeth and drove off.

Two hours later and all of us except Harry were clustered under a large tree on the edge of a motorway café. The sky was overcast and a light drizzle pattered onto the leaves above us.

251

I glanced over at Harry. He was squatting under a neighbouring tree, Ed's laptop in his hands. He didn't appear to be paying any attention to our conversation.

Not that anyone was speaking right now. In fact, a heavy silence hung over the group. Ketty – who hadn't needed stitches, but who was still pale and limping from the bite on her leg – was the first to break it.

'So we're decided, then?'

'It's the only way,' Nico said. 'The only way we'll be safe.'

Laura nodded. She'd been resistant at first, but after we'd explained how we'd seen – and then lost – the proof against Geri, she accepted our decision. After all, if we turned ourselves over to the authorities, we would just end up in Geri's hands.

'I'll call ahead and find you somewhere to stay tonight,' Laura said. 'Will you let me know when you get there?'

'Of course,' I reassured her. 'Once we're out of the country, everything will get easier.'

Laura hurried away from the tree to make the call.

Our plan was to smuggle ourselves on a ferry to France and head along the coast to wherever Laura managed to book for us – a place for us to hide out for a few days and work out where on earth we went next.

It wasn't what I wanted.

At last I knew who killed my parents – but, instead of being able to take revenge, I was running away.

Now that I'd had a little time to think, I could hardly

contain the loathing I felt for Geri. Knowing what she'd done to my mom and dad was bad enough, but when I thought about her lies and deceit . . . the way she'd pretended she was my friend . . . confided in me . . . a terrible fury consumed me and all I could think about was hurting her in some way.

'Guys?' Harry appeared, Ed's laptop tucked under his arm. 'I think I've found something.'

'What?' Ed asked.

Harry glanced at his mother. She was still busy with her phone call. He lowered his voice and turned to me. 'D'you remember last night Geri said that she killed your dad because he was threatening to reveal something?'

I nodded, a fresh wave of rage flowing through me as I thought back to the conversation and Geri's smug, arrogant attitude.

'And d'you remember those five meetings your dad had with Bookman in the week before he died and how I downloaded the notes that had been logged on those meetings?'

'Course we do,' Nico said impatiently. 'What have you found?'

'I've just managed to decrypt the files from those meetings and there's something interesting,' Harry said.

'What?' I stared at him anxiously. With everything that had happened I'd completely forgotten about the meetings between my dad and Bookman.

'Most of it just backs up what Geri said about William – your dad – threatening to expose her latest project. All the references to what William wanted to expose have been deleted, except in one place,' Harry said eagerly. 'It's the last conversation William Fox had with Bookman. It doesn't make any sense on its own, but if you understand the context . . .'

He handed me the open laptop and pointed to the screen. I read the email out loud.

No more discussion. If the code goes to Sydney, I go to the police.

'The code's the Medusa code obviously,' Nico said.

'Yes, my dad was threatening to tell the police if Bookman gave it to this guy Sydney,' I said.

'I didn't think anyone else other than William Fox *had* the code before he died,' Laura said. 'Bookman and Geri must have stolen it.'

'But if Geri stole the code years ago you'd have thought she'd have kept a copy before selling it to Sydney,' Ed mused. 'In which case, why was she so desperate to get hold of that copy William Fox left with his brother?'

No one had an answer to that.

'At least we know why Geri killed my dad,' I said. 'To stop him exposing the fact that she and Bookman were giving the code to Sydney.'

'Who's Sydney?' Ed asked.

'I don't know.' I frowned.

'And why would William risk his own life to tell the police about Sydney having the code?' Nico said.

'Because he knew it killed our mothers,' Ketty breathed. 'And he didn't want it used again.'

Silence fell, the only sound the soft pattering of the rain above our heads.

'D'you think they did it?' I said. 'I mean, d'you think Bookman and Geri really gave the Medusa code to Sydney?'

I caught Ed's eye. I could see he understood where my thoughts were headed.

'Man, if they did . . .' Nico said.

'. . . Then there might be others,' Ketty added. 'Others like us . . . with the Medusa gene.'

Exactly.

I stared at the grey sky in the distance. Another shock, in a day full of them. For as long as I'd known about the Medusa gene, there had only ever been the four of us.

'Others with the gene means others with psychic powers,' Ed said.

'And dead mothers,' Ketty added.

'We have to find out,' I said.

I might not be in a position to take revenge on Geri, but I could at least try to find out what my father had died attempting to stop.

'But we don't know who Sydney is or where to find him,' Ed said. 'He might be dead. He might be dangerous. And if the code for the Medusa gene did change hands, it happened fifteen years ago . . . the trail will be completely cold by now . . .'

'I know it won't be easy,' I said. 'But there are people who can help us.' I threw a glance at Harry. 'You're a good hacker,' I said. 'Having you on the end of the phone could make all the difference.'

Harry stared at me. I couldn't read his look.

Laura walked over. 'I've booked you into a hotel in France. It's near the place where the ferry docks and it's paid for in advance. It shouldn't be hard to find. I've texted you the details, Dylan.'

Ed cleared his throat. 'Geri might believe for a while that Dylan and Nico died in the blast, but eventually the forensics will show there are no bodies in the rubble,' he said. 'Which means the sooner we leave the better.'

'I'll take you to the docks,' Laura said.

'No,' Nico said. 'I mean, we're all grateful for your help, but if anyone sees us together, you and Harry could become targets.'

Laura opened her mouth to protest, but I spoke first.

'We need you here, in the UK,' I said. 'Any taxi can take us to the docks, but you're the only people here we can trust, which is much more important. Please.'

Laura closed her mouth and let out a long, shaky breath. 'Okay, I'll call you a cab.' She took out her phone.

The rain fell more heavily. I could feel it on my hair and neck. I reached out and touched Laura's arm, sending my protective force around us both.

I couldn't believe how simple it was, once I stopped trying so hard to control the energy.

Laura smiled, suddenly aware that the rain was no longer falling on her head.

After the call, she drew me to one side. 'I can't bear to lose you having only just found you,' she said. 'But I can see it's for the best. Geri Paterson is too powerful to take chances with.' She paused. 'I want to thank you. When Harry told me how you saved him and Nico, I didn't know whether to shout at him for coming after you or hug you for protecting him.'

'Harry saved me, too,' I said, glancing round to make sure he wasn't in earshot. 'He worked out about the gas. If we hadn't known about that so early on, I might not have had enough time to get out of the room.'

'When's the cab coming?' Nico wandered over. 'Laura and Harry should go before it gets here. We don't want anyone to connect us to them.'

'It'll be here in a few minutes,' Laura said. 'I want to stay, make sure you get off okay.'

'No, please. Nico's right,' I said. 'You should go.'

'Okay.' Laura gave me a hug, then went back to the others. 'Come on, Harry. We can call later.'

I watched her and Harry saying goodbye to Nico, Ketty and Ed. As Laura walked over to her car, I stared at the damp grass, bracing myself.

Harry was about to leave.

And then he walked right up to me. 'Hey, Red,' he said. 'Come with me for a sec.'

I could feel Nico, Ed and Ketty staring at us, but I kept

my eyes on Harry, following him past the trees and into a clearing near some large bushes. As soon as we were out of sight, Harry grabbed my hand. My stomach flipped over.

'I could come with you, Red,' he said. 'I can hack into IT systems . . . I can be useful . . .'

'I know,' I said. 'But you have to stay with your mom. She needs you. And you can be useful here, too.'

Harry shook his head. He smiled. He dropped my hand and dug into his pocket. 'Well, at least take this.' Harry took the Clusterchaos program and pressed it into my palm. 'I can get another copy . . . I've shown Ed how to use it. He can tell the rest of you.'

I nodded. 'Thank you.'

'Harry! We should go,' Laura called.

'Coming!' Harry took a step away from me. 'I'll miss you, Red.'

'Wait.'

Harry stopped.

I swallowed. 'I'm sorry I was rude to you . . . before. I didn't think . . . I mean, *I* thought Jack was amazing when I met him . . . and he's your dad. I can understand why you got caught up in his—'

'No, there's *no* excuse,' Harry said bitterly. 'I can't believe I thought Jack was so cool . . .' He paused. '. . . I can't believe I let him make me lie to someone I really like . . .'

He stopped and a silence fell between us. The rain started to fall harder again. Instinctively, I summoned my force field to stop the rain from reaching me. In the background I could hear Laura's car door slam shut and the others talking in a low murmur.

I moved closer to Harry. 'When you say . . . about the someone you really like . . . is that . . . do you mean . . .?'

'You, Red.' Harry took a step towards me. He grinned. 'Obviously, I mean you.'

We were standing right in front of each other now.

'You think you're real cute, don't you?' I raised my eyebrows.

'I think you think I am.' Harry's grin split his face.

He bent down so our faces were almost touching.

And then I let the force field around me slide away and we kissed.

It seemed to go on forever, but it couldn't have been more than a few seconds. We drew away from each other. Harry blew out his breath.

'We are so doing that again,' he said.

'Yeah,' I said. 'Real soon.'

He squeezed my hand, then we walked through the trees and out to Laura's car. She waved at me as Harry got in beside her. Seconds later they were gone.

I stared after them, along the empty road. The rain was falling more heavily now, drops running down my face. I didn't bother to engage my force field.

Instead, I stood in the rain. Alone.

After all my efforts to find out what really happened to my parents, what was I left with?

I'd lost the only proof that Geri Paterson killed my parents – and both she and Jack were still at large and unpunished while I was forced to flee the country.

The copy of the Medusa code my dad had left me was buried in a remote garden and – even if I was ever able to come back here to reclaim it – I didn't have a clue what I was supposed to do with it.

And, just as Laura and Harry came into my life, they were gone.

Nico and Ketty appeared on either side of me.

I glanced at them. 'What?'

'I like the guy,' Nico said with a grin. 'What about you, Ketts?'

'Harry?' Ketty said. 'Sure I like him. He's cool. I wonder how Dylan feels?'

'Don't either of you even think about making fun of me,' I snarled. 'I'm not in the freakin' mood.'

'I wouldn't dream of doing such a thing,' Nico said archly.

'Me neither,' Ketty added. 'I mean, it's not every day you see people fall in love. It's kind of a special thing.'

'I'm not in—' I stopped, knowing that getting defensive would just make me look like I was lying . . . knowing, in my heart, that denial *was* a lie . . .

'Whatever . . .' Nico chuckled. 'Hey, maybe having a boyfriend will soften Dylan up a bit.'

'If you don't shut up, I'll soften *you* up a bit,' I growled.

'She doesn't sound softer, does she?' Ketty giggled.

'I like her lacking in softness,' Ed said with a smile, wandering over. 'It's what I'm used to.'

A car pulled round the corner and a tired-looking, grey-haired man leaned out of the window. 'You kids call a cab?' he shouted.

We headed to the taxi.

'I call shotgun,' I grunted. 'By which I mean I want to sit in the front seat . . . as far away from you guys as I can get.'

'Fine with me,' Nico said. 'You can sit where you like. I owe you for saving my life.'

'And me,' Ketty said. 'Feel the love, Dylan.'

Ed grinned. 'Looks like you're stuck with it.'

'Three friends and a boyfriend,' Ketty laughed.

'And all being nice to you in one day,' Nico added.

'Oh, bite me,' I said.

And, trying not to let them see me the smile that, in spite of everything, was creeping across my face, I got into the front seat of the cab and we drove away, into our new future.

To be continued in . . . *DOUBLE-CROSS*

LOOK OUT FOR THE FINAL TWO CHAPTERS IN THE MEDUSA PROJECT SERIES!

COMING JULY 2021

HAVE YOU READ THE FIRST THREE ADVENTURES IN THIS THRILLING SERIES?

LOVE THE MEDUSA PROJECT?
LOOK OUT FOR SOPHIE MCKENZIE'S
BESTSELLING MISSING TRILOGY